HIDDEN TREASURE, MOB BOSSES, AND A TICKING CLOCK

"So it *is* the art you want," I said, triumphant. Two could play the "get under your skin" game. "Thanks for confirming."

"Of course that's what it is, genius. And Sully will do whatever it takes to get his hands on it. Or is that 'take whatever he wants' to get his hands on it?" She cocked an eyebrow at me. "Maybe I should spend some time with your mommy or grammy, and see if they can help me find them?" She pushed off from the gate.

Mom and Nini? I couldn't let them get involved in this. What if they got hurt? They were all I had.

"Don't you go *near* them," I growled, forcing strength into my voice that I didn't feel. "I'll get the paintings for you. Promise."

The Redhead gave me a slow, predatory smile, and headed down the street in the opposite direction. After a few long steps she turned and waggled her fingers at me. "Do it. You have ten days, sweetheart."

I turned to Ollie, who was pale, but had a determined expression on his face.

"Psycho," he whispered. "Forg
Mox. We've got work to do."

OTHER BOOKS YOU MAY ENJOY

MOXIE

and the art of

RULE
BREAKING

ERIN
DIONNE

A 14-DAY MYSTERY

PUFFIN BOOKS
An Imprint of Penguin Group (USA)

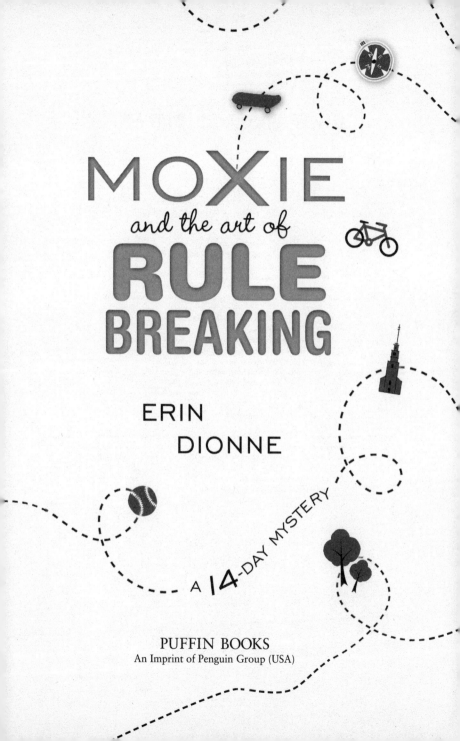

PUFFIN BOOKS
Published by the Penguin Group
Penguin Group (USA) LLC
375 Hudson Street
New York, New York 10014

USA * Canada * UK * Ireland * Australia
New Zealand * India * South Africa * China

penguin.com
A Penguin Random House Company

First published in the United States of America by Dial Books for Youmg Readers,
a division of Penguin Young Readers Group, 2013
Published by Puffin Books, an imprint of Penguin Young Readers Group, 2014

THE LIBRARY OF CONGRESS HAS CATALOGED THE DIAL BOOKS EDITION AS FOLLOWS:
Dionne, Erin, date.
Moxie and the art of rule breaking: a 14-day mystery / Erin Dionne.
pages cm
Summary: Instead of spending a carefree summer exploring downtown Boston with best friend Ollie, thirteen-
year-old Moxie must solve a famous art heist in order to protect those she loves from her ailing grandfather's
gangster past. Includes facts about the 1990 Gardner Museum art theft. Includes bibliographical resources (p. 249).
ISBN 978-0-8037-3871-3 (hardcover)
[1. Grandfathers—Fiction. 2. Art thefts—Fiction. 3. Gangsters—Fiction.
4. Boston (Mass.)—Fiction. 5. Mystery and detective stories.] I. Title
PZ7.D6216Wr 2013
[Fic]—dc23
2012022306

Puffin Books ISBN 978-0-14-242614-2

Printed in the United States of America

1 3 5 7 9 10 8 6 4 2

For Big Pip, Dudge, and grandfathers and granddaughters everywhere

MOXIE

and the art of

RULE BREAKING

1

You know that line about being "saved by the bell"? Well, it's a lie.

The events that ruined not only what was supposed to be the best summer ever, but my family *and* life as I knew it, began with a bell: a ringing doorbell.

See, that summer was the last one that my best friend, Ollie, and I would be together before we split to go to different high schools—and everyone knows that even though people say they're going to hang out and still be friends and do stuff together, that doesn't really happen. Social gravity pulls you to your new group: He'd be hanging out with the guys at Chestnut College Prep, and I'd be halfway across town at Boston Classics. But the summer? That was ours.

Anyway, when the whole "bell ruining my life" thing happened, I was working on the final set of geometry proofs of the school year and rockin' to The Standells' song about Boston, "Dirty Water"—perfect for late afternoon, neighbor-annoying, open window blaring.

Assuming it was Mom—who forgets her keys as often as I forget my cell phone—and not a life-altering visitor, I tucked my pencil into the textbook, banged down the stairs from my room yelling "Hold on!" and bolted through our apartment to the house's front door. The doorbell rang again.

I didn't bother to check the peephole or anything, just threw it open while saying "Mom, do I have to have dinner with you and—"

It wasn't my mom. I had never seen this woman before in my life. And her being not-Mom surprised me so much that words bottlenecked in my throat, and I stared. She had:

Red hair—dark and long, it was probably dyed, but whoever did it knew what they were doing, because it was an awesome, uniform color, not like Jolie Pearson's, this idiot girl in my grade who pretends she's a blond when she's clearly, streakily, not.

Black skinny jeans and leather jacket—even though it was close to eighty degrees and way too hot for any coat.

Pale skin. Dark eyes. Staring straight at me, waiting.

Ever since I was nine, as long as my grandparents were in their downstairs apartment, my mom left me home alone. I had strict instructions not to open the door to anyone I didn't know—it was one of our sacred family rules. And I'd always been good about following it.

Well, until now.

The door was thrown wide. I couldn't just slam it in her face and call a do-over. She didn't look sketchy . . . but you could never be too careful about these things. I leaned against the frame, hoping for a "no way, that wasn't me who just banged down the stairs and shouted through the door calling you Mom" vibe.

"Can I help you?" I asked, brain and mouth finally in gear.

"Is Joe here?" she asked. Her glance flicked behind me to the door of my grandma's apartment, then up to mine. I'd left it open. The Standells were yelling "Aaww-aaww, Boston you're my home" from my third-floor bedroom.

"Joe?" I repeated, not sure who she meant. The Redhead leaned forward slightly, as if she was trying to see around me.

"Joe Burke."

She was looking for my grandpa, Grumps.

Opening that door? Total tactical error.

Grumps was the same place he'd been for the past two years: Alton Rivers Care facility. He had Alzheimer's and my grandma Nini, Mom, and I couldn't care for him at home anymore.

My hands went cold. It hadn't happened in years, but strangers used to come looking for my grandfather all the time. See, Grumps, besides being the greatest grandpa in the universe, is something else. Or *was*, before the Alzheimer's. Some called him a "made man," some called him "part of the crew." He called himself "a specialist." But any way you say it, it means one thing:

Grumps was a criminal.

I changed my mind: Redhead = beautiful, but definitely sketchy.

"No," I answered.

"Will he be back soon?" she asked. Her voice was buttery,

but her hard eyes were focused over my head at Nini's door, not even pretending to acknowledge me. So rude.

"Dunno," I said, stuffing every bit of uninterested teen attitude that I could into the word. Then I waited. Her over-my-head gaze didn't change. My heart thudded. Why had it been me who'd opened the door?

"Well," she said, and brought her eyes to mine. They oozed . . . what was that word? Words are not my thing, numbers are. But we had to memorize vocab lists last year in language arts for some standardized test, and Ollie and I competed to see who could learn the most. And this one was on there . . . Contempt! That was it. *Contempt*. Like I was such a disgusting waste of her time, she couldn't believe she had to speak to me. And that I probably couldn't even understand what she was saying.

She leaned down, her face so close to mine, I could smell the cigarettes on her breath, and stuck a long, perfectly manicured, dark-polished fingernail into my chest. And she pushed me, hard. I snagged the frame to keep steady as fear streaked through me. This chick was *way* more than sketchy.

"Since you 'dunno,' maybe you could find out. Tell your mommy or grammy or whoever that Sully Cupcakes is looking for him. I'll wait." She straightened and crossed her arms.

That pushing and arm-crossing totally ticked me off.

I cocked my head at her. "Sorry," I said, anger smothering the fear-streak from seconds ago, "they're out too. And I probably shouldn't be talking to a *stray*-nger." I made it sound as sickly sweet as I could and stepped back into the house, about to close the door.

She stuck a black leather high-heeled boot out to block it. "You have lousy manners," she snapped.

I just raised an eyebrow and didn't say anything—something that drives my mom absolutely berserk—and hoped I seemed cooler than I felt. Who wears black leather boots in the summer, anyway?

I could almost see the steam coming out her ears. And for a moment, I wondered if I was in over my head. But I pushed that thought down the turnpike, as Nini would say. I knew plenty of guys from the "crews" that Grumps had worked with over the years—one of them, Little Joey Colagionne, who'd gotten me hooked on classic Boston punk and rock bands, was like an uncle to me—and this redhead and Sully Cupcakes weren't part of them. There was absolutely no reason to tell her the truth about Grumps.

"Fine," she snarled, and turned on her heel. Her hair whiffed by my nose, trailing the smell of cigarettes and cut grass. In spite of myself, I flinched. And was immediately mad that I did.

"Can I take a message?" I added, going for the last word.

She stomped down the stairs like she hadn't heard me. At the bottom she paused, then turned and gave me a shark-smile.

"Yeah. Sully Cupcakes wants his items back. By the fourth. Or he'll take something of equal . . ." She paused and looked me up and down, real slow. "... or *lesser* value." I waited until she closed the front gate, then I shut the house door and double locked it.

Sketchy? Nah.

Total psycho.

2

I'd just finished twisting the lock when Nini came out of her apartment, wearing one of her classic Red Sox jerseys, asking who'd been ringing the doorbell. The sounds of today's game—the afternoon part of a double header—trailed from her open door.

"Wilderness Scouts," I lied, because I didn't want to get in trouble for opening the door to a psychotic redheaded stranger. "They were selling candy."

"They do that in November. Who was it?" Her sharp green eyes don't miss much. She pointedly glanced at my empty, slightly shaking hands. I stuffed them in my skirt's pockets and tried again.

"Just some kids selling stuff. No big deal."

She crossed her arms and frowned at me, eyebrows drawn down and head cocked. I call her No-Nonsense Nini when she makes that face.

"Seriously!" I said, hoping that sounding annoyed would convince her.

It worked. Nini eyed me up and down one more time and disappeared back into her apartment, probably to shout at the Sox.

My breath was coming fast and the back of my neck tingled. I hate lying. I sat on the stairs to chill.

Grumps hadn't been involved in "the lifestyle," as he called it, for years. Well, obviously because of the Alzheimer's, but he'd retired right after I was born. Said I was more precious than the work he did with the crews. Mom rolled her eyes when she heard that. Whatever. She's just jealous of how tight we are.

Grumps and I are so tight, he gave me my nickname—Moxie—and I gave him his. Mine is from this soda he liked as a kid that had a bright orange label that Ted Williams, from the Red Sox, used to promote. If it weren't for him, everyone would be calling me Margaret Mildred, or something awful like "Peg" or "Midge." And I named him Grumps because as a baby I couldn't say "Grampy," which is what he wanted to be called. So "grampy" became "grumpy," became "grumps." I know it's totally goofy, but what can you do? I was, like, three.

Anyway, even when he was involved in the lifestyle, he wasn't a major player. At least, that's what he told me. He was a carpenter, and carpenters come in handy when you need places to hide stuff—like money. Or jewelry. Or whatever. So he made "modifications" to a few guys' houses . . . and occasionally held cash for them when things got heavy. It was all small-time, he said. He never hurt anyone and never actually stole anything himself. So Grumps had hidden something for this Sully guy, but what? And when? 'Cause it had to have been tucked away since I was a baby.

I'm sure it'd freak most people out if they knew that my criminal grandfather told his granddaughter about his shady past. But Grumps was big on being honest with me, and made it clear that I was never, ever to get involved with any kind of street life—he said it'd limit my potential. Instead, he pushed me to do well in school and helped me with my math homework every night. Because of him, I wanted to be on the other side of the law, like a code breaker. Or a forensic psychologist—one of those people who testify in court about how long a criminal should be sentenced and why they do what they do.

So although I don't agree with what Grumps did all those years ago, he's still my grandpa, I love him like crazy, and I wouldn't want him to go to jail. Besides, once the Alzheimer's kicked in, what he used to be didn't matter much anymore.

I double-checked the locks on the front door and headed upstairs. My geometry homework had lost its appeal—as had The Standells. Instead, I turned on some Aerosmith and booted up our computer. Time for a little Google-fu to find out about Sully and what he'd want with Grumps.

I typed in "Sully Cupcakes."

About 2,142,367 results. And, based on the first dozen or so, Sully Cupcakes was not a small-time guy:

The Search for Boston Gangster James "Sully Cupcakes" O'Sullivan Continues
Boston Mobster Sully Cupcakes Scheduled to Appear in Court
James "Sully Cupcakes" O'Sullivan: an online encyclopedia article.

Why hadn't I heard about him? Before the Alzheimer's, Grumps told me occasional stories about the characters on the scene.

I clicked back to the first page of results and launched the encyclopedia entry.

The attached photo was of this dark-haired guy built like a refrigerator with eyes that would scare a snake. "Sully Cupcakes" earned his sweet nickname because he planned most of his jobs from the back of a bakery. According to the site, he'd committed nearly every crime from stealing to murder and whatever fell in between. He'd been in some big federal prison in Tennessee since I was a little kid, and had recently gotten out.

Oh.

Maybe that's why I hadn't heard of him?

Had Grumps seriously been involved with this guy?

I skimmed Sully Cupcakes' biography and the bit about the life he'd set up so no one knew he was a crook—bakery owner, husband, dad, the usual. Then came a list of the crimes he'd committed. There were so many, I had to scroll down the page to see them all. At the bottom of that was a second list—this one of "alleged involvement." The article said Sully Cupcakes may have participated in a bunch of other crimes, but no one could prove it—yet. I checked the list: more murders, racketeering, and extortion, which is basically bullying people for money

What had he sent the grouchy redhead to find? And why did he want it back by the fourth? I guessed she meant the Fourth of July, which was two weeks away.

I clicked through some other articles, hoping to find out more about him, but they all said essentially the same thing: Sully was a bad guy who did bad things and hung out with bad people. As I thought about what he wanted, in my head I heard Grumps talking me through word problems when I struggled with them years ago.

"You need information to solve this. Do you have everything you need, Moxie?" he'd say gently. That was usually a clue that I was missing something. I'd go back through the problem and figure out the missing piece. Once I had all the data, I could do the work easily. But until then, it was like something I couldn't grab dancing at the edges of my brain. This felt the same way. No matter what info I read about Sully Cupcakes, a part remained out of reach. I closed my eyes and rocked back, balancing my chair on its rear legs, thinking.

What if I told Nini or Mom about this?

There was only one answer to that: No. No way. Negatory. They might freak out and go into lockdown mode or something—and that would wreck my "best summer ever" plans with Ollie: No Sox games, beach time, or exploring Boston. Nope. If this was legit, I was going to deal with it solo.

On the other hand, should I even take her seriously? I mean, who threatens a thirteen-year-old and demands they find stolen "items"?

But was it worth it to take the chance that it was a joke? Sully Cupcakes *was* a real person, and Grumps knew some shady characters . . .

I was concentrating so hard on the problem, I nearly fell over backward when my phone rang.

3

"Yeah?" I barked into the phone, struggling to get my act together and not scoping my caller ID.

"Nice manners, Mox."

Ollie. Thanks to a double-booked babysitter, we'd been best friends since second grade. Through the whole "girls and boys can't be friends" thing in fifth and sixth grade when we didn't hang out at all at school, Nini watched Ollie when we got home. We did our homework and watched bad sci-fi movies together, and that was it: He was like my fairly cool, allergy-ridden, younger-by-two-months brother. Our families did a lot of stuff together too—celebrating birthdays and a few holidays and whatnot. That whole "joined at the hip" saying? Yeah. Us.

Besides, I didn't fit in with the girls in my class—I had no interest in the nail polish and shiny hair crowd, the readers and theater girls couldn't get their brains around my love for math, and sports weren't my thing. Whatever. No biggie—I had Ollie.

He didn't fit in either. His asthma and chubbiness kept him from athletics, which were big at our school. Most of his guy friends were in his Wilderness Scout troop, but they went to other junior highs. That's part of the reason he was going to Chestnut College Prep—to hang with his friends and give his big brain more room to grow.

At least I'd have Ollie till the fall. And even though we lived close by and hung out whenever we could, I wasn't stupid: Things were going to change. And that was *not* cool.

"Sorry," I said, and let out a whoosh of air, annoyed at my jumpiness.

"Hey—oh." He stopped. "'Seasons of Wither'?! Seriously?"

"Huh—? Oh. Yeah," I said, clueing in to the Aerosmith song filling my room.

"Isn't that a little *out* of season?"

"Good music is *never* out of season," I snapped, my tone harsher than I intended . . . even though he was right. The song was written about Massachusetts winters, and this early summer day was anything but snowy and depressing. "It's an Aerosmith playlist," I tried again. "Just what happened to come up."

"Cool. Hey—did you talk to your mom yet? I want to head over to the Arboretum before it gets dark, and my parents won't let me go alone." Earlier that afternoon Ollie'd texted me about hitting the park, but my mom wanted me to have dinner with her and her boyfriend, Putrid Richard. Which was what I was going to ask her if I could skip when I raced downstairs and opened the door to Ms. Redhead.

I hate having dinner with them. Mom spends most of the

meal giggling at his lame jokes and work stories, while I spend most of it skeeving over the food flecks stuck in his mustache. He does something at the national parks office downtown and has to deal with tourists who say and do ridiculous things. Some of the stuff he tells us is pretty funny—like the family from Nebraska who wanted a refund after seeing the USS *Constitution* because they expected the real, paper, Constitution to be there (hint: Our *Constitution* is a boat)—but most of the stories aren't. Mom doesn't share many funny work stories. She works as a receptionist for a local funeral home. Seriously.

But lately, Putrid Richard has done a lot of talking about how much he loves New Hampshire, how quiet and beautiful it is, how awesome it is to observe nature up there; and I sensed more changes coming my way. Seriously unacceptable, one state over, changes. Changes that would make Ollie and me going to different schools seem like no big deal.

"Haven't talked to her yet. You on another hunt?" Ollie was big into geocaching—or "urban treasure hunting," as he called it. He tracked down treasure boxes in random places around town using a handheld GPS and a list of coordinates off the web. There wasn't actual treasure in the boxes—just pins and weird bottle caps and whatever—but every time Ollie logged another cache it was like he'd discovered a chest of gold. It made him happy, which was awesome, but didn't do much for me. Figuring out where the stuff was seemed more exciting, and if you already had the coordinates, well . . . what's the fun in that?

But Ollie told me that it's all about what you *see*, and how you look for things. "It's a lot harder to see what's really around you than you might think," he told me once. I'm not sure I got it.

"How'd you know?" he said. "This one should be tough. The guy who hid it, GI Goh, has done some of the best caches I've found . . ." He went on, talking about boxes disguised as rocks and one in the Public Garden, but all I heard were the Sully Cupcakes details rattling around in my head. Ollie didn't know about Grumps's less-than-honest past—another sacred family rule was to keep family business to ourselves—and I didn't want him asking questions I couldn't answer.

"If my mom lets me, I'll go," I told him, which was basically what I'd texted him when I got home. I'd rather hang with Ollie than Putrid Richard anytime.

"Something bugging you, Mox?" he said.

"Why?" My heart picked up speed. Since he was usually buried in his GPS or attached to a video game controller, Ollie wasn't the best at reading people, but when he latched on to something . . .

"Number one," he said, and I could imagine him pushing up his glasses, then ticking the reasons off on his fingers. "You haven't made a crack about the geocache, and number two, you never listen to 'Seasons of Wither' after the snow melts, regardless of whether or not it comes up in a playlist."

Ollie knows me better than anyone.

"Disco," I answered.

"Wha . . . ?" he said. "Oh. Is this Moxie-lingo?"

I laughed. "Disco!" I repeated. "Sounds good as a response to anything, doesn't it?"

"The word sounds way better than the music ever did," Ollie muttered.

The call-waiting on my phone clicked. My mom. Bell saving was *not* happening for me. I was supposed to call her when I got home but was, uh, distracted. "My mom's beeping in. I'll text you when I know what's going on."

"Disco," said Ollie. I grinned and switched over to Mom's call.

"My battery ran out," I said, anticipating her lecture, "and I already made plans with Ollie."

"Well, Richard and I want to have dinner with you tonight," she said. "There are a few things that we need to discuss." I covered the mouthpiece on the phone and groaned. Mom had her "I won't take no for an answer" voice on. I'd like to see *her* in a room with Sully Cupcakes. She could totally take him.

"Oh-kay," I groaned, stretching the word out. "What time and where?"

She gave me the details—we'd be going to one of my favorite restaurants—and as she spoke, something occurred to me.

"Can you pick me up at Alton Rivers?" I asked her.

"I guess," she said. "But isn't it late for you to be heading over there?"

I glanced at the clock. "If I hop on my bike, I can be there before they have dinner," I said. "I missed my regular visit because of end-of-the-year stuff."

She warned me that Grumps might not be in a good

place—Nini would have been in this morning, and visitors take a lot out of him—but said sure, I could go.

I clicked off with Mom, then texted Ollie that I'd have to bail on the Arboretum. I tossed a hoodie, my wallet, keys, and cell phone into my backpack, killed Aerosmith, and headed downstairs to say bye to Nini.

More data, here I come.

4

The colorful shopping area of Jamaica Plain, the Boston neighborhood where my family lives, blurred by as I dodged clueless pedestrians and distracted drivers on the way to Alton Rivers.

A few minutes later, I clicked my bike to the rack outside the facility. I'm not sure why they had a bike rack out there—mine was the only one I ever saw on it—but I appreciated it. It'd totally suck to come outside from visiting a relative in a nursing home and find that someone jacked your ride.

Inside, Iris, the elderly desk monitor who likes big jewelry and buckets of flowery perfume, quizzed me about summer vacation and the "big move to high school" while I signed in, my eyes watering from her olfactory assault. I tried to be polite—summer in the city and Boston Classics High next year . . . yes it'd be exciting to attend such a prestigious school, no I didn't mind the uniform (which was a total lie—around the house I referred to the plaid jumper as the Uniform of Horror) blah blah blah . . . But my brain buzzed with questions for Grumps.

"It's been great talking with you, Iris," I told her, "but I've gotta find Grumps before dinner. Do you know where he is?"

"Try his room, love," she said. She blew me a kiss and I headed down the main hall, relieved to breathe fresh air.

Alton Rivers is nice for a nursing home, I guess—not that I'm an expert or anything. There are big windows that overlook a backyard garden, the walls are painted a light yellow, and it smells like lemons, not old people.

I checked Grumps's room, but he wasn't there. I dropped off my backpack and helmet and headed to the back porch—his second-favorite spot to hang out in the afternoons. I saw him before he saw me.

He was parked in his wheelchair in the sun, back to me, his dandelion fluff of white hair waving in the light breeze, and my heart broke a little, just like it did every time I arrived. I walked around to the front of the chair and squatted down, holding my breath. The first minute was the worst—you never knew what you were going to get. All of the Sully Cupcakes questions were replaced with the same ones I think every time I visit: Will he recognize me today? Is it a good memory day?

"Hey, Grumps!" I said, giving him a big smile.

His bright blue eyes lit up under his bushy eyebrows.

"Moxie-girl!" he said. All the air whooshed out of me as I gave him a hug.

A confused expression flitted over his face, and he frowned.

"I don't have any pudding," he said.

On Wednesdays, when I usually visit, the cafeteria at Alton Rivers serves butterscotch pudding for dessert after lunch, and if Grumps is having a good memory day, he saves his for me. Butterscotch is my favorite. Evidently, today was an off-the-charts great memory day.

"Surprise! It's Thursday," I said, and grinned. I dragged a deck chair over and plopped into it. "But my schedule has been crazy with the last day of school tomorrow, and I wanted to make sure I saw you this week." And see if I could get information about this mysterious redhead who showed up at our house today.

Grumps smiled. "Checkers?"

We always do the same thing when I visit: Hang out on the big sunny porch and play checkers. Grumps never played checkers before his diagnosis, but the docs say it's a good activity for his brain and he seems to like it. Sometimes I have to remind him if his pieces are black or red, but other than that he does pretty well. He beats me most of the time, but that's good. If I start winning too many games, I'll start to worry about him more than I already do.

I checked the clock over the door. Plenty of time for a game before dinner.

"I'll get the board." I went inside and grabbed a checkers set off the rack in the rec room, then set up the pieces.

I spent a few minutes enjoying the game, trying not to think about The Redhead and Sully Cupcakes, or who Grumps used to be before Alzheimer's and after his criminal past.

When our game was almost finished, Grumps paused to watch this red bird do its bird thing in the feeder that hangs from the tree just outside the back door. I watched Grumps watch the bird, and it was time to ask.

"Grumps . . ." I trailed off. He turned to me, as alert as I'd seen him in weeks. My insides squeezed. Asking him about the past was risky. He could drift.

But I had to know. I swallowed hard.

"Grumps, do you remember anyone named Sully?"

A shadow flitted across his eyes. His hands—he has these huge hands—shook. Just a little. Not slosh-coffee-down-your-pants shaking, but more like ripples-across-the-top-of-the-cup shaking. They'd never done that before.

"I know a lot of Sullys," he answered.

That was probably true. Sully is a nickname for Sullivan, and, if you live in Boston like we do, Sullivans are as common as Dunkin' Donuts coffee shops.

Honesty, right?

"Sully Cupcakes?"

His eyes narrowed to slits just like the way my mom's do when she's angry over something I said about Putrid Richard.

"Where'd you hear that name?" A vein popped out on his forehead, which is probably a very bad sign when you're eighty-three and have Alzheimer's.

I swallowed again. "I saw it online," I said, losing my nerve and lying—for . . . what? The third time this afternoon?

"Well, forget it," he said. "Bad news, that one."

Obviously.

"Did you ever work with him?"

This time, Grumps didn't answer, just pressed his lips

together and stared out across the garden. I didn't want to believe it, but the quick stab to my heart told me *yes*. Grumps didn't lie to me. I wished I could blame this on his disease, but deep down, I knew: Grumps was avoiding the truth. On purpose. And he was aware that he was doing it.

Before I could ask another question, the back door opened and Angel, his aide, came out to the porch.

"Moxie!" he cried. "What a surprise!"

Angel is young—once he told me that he works at ARC to help pay for nursing school—and has these amazing dark brown eyes and a dimple in his left cheek. And really big biceps, from lifting people in and out of wheelchairs so much, I guess. I try to remember that he's a medical professional, but his hotness can be distracting.

Angel retrieved a blanket from the pocket on the back of Grumps's wheelchair and spread it over his legs. I turned away, struggling with what this latest change—Grumps avoiding me—meant. Over the past two years, I'd watched a lot of things around Grumps change: what he could do for himself, what we could do together, and—maybe the saddest change—what we could do for him. But even though all those other parts of life around Grumps had changed, our relationship had stayed steady. Or I thought it had.

Now? I had no idea what was the truth and what was a lie.

"Time for dinner, Mr. Burke," he said. Grumps grunted.

Angel released the brake on Grumps's chair and I got up to hold the door for them. Grumps cruised by me, not meeting my gaze.

5

Still stinging from Grumps's omission, I said bye to Iris and found Mom's tiny hatchback parked outside of Alton Rivers, engine idling. I pushed away a flare of annoyance that she hadn't come in and said hello. Instead, I snuck up to the passenger-side door and peeked through the window at her: head bent over her notebook, scribbling away. Mom makes lists like other people breathe—all the time. She has this square chubby notebook with about five hundred pages in it, and that's where she keeps everything she has to do, I have to do, things she might want to do, or what I should be doing in my free time. I tapped on the glass and she jumped. She leaned over and unlocked the door, then popped the back. I wrestled my bike in, struggling with the handlebars, then slid into the front seat.

"Hey, honey." She pecked me on the cheek. "How was he?" she asked, eyes on the floor.

I shrugged, not wanting to give her the satisfaction of a full report. She hadn't been to visit in at least two weeks. Of the three of us, Mom visits Grumps the least. She says it's really hard to watch him slipping away and she "just can't do it." But—

hello!—it's hard for me and Nini too, and we go. I pointed out that if she saw him more often, the changes would feel more gradual. She didn't like hearing that. Basically, she likes to move forward, and Alzheimer's doesn't allow that—at least, that's what Angel's told me. He's talked to her about it a few times.

Her lips tightened into a thin line and she put the car in gear, then pulled into traffic.

"Richard is looking forward to seeing you," she said. I rolled my eyes and stared out the window. "You should give him a chance, you know."

More staring. I'd heard this a zillion times before and I *had* given Richard a chance. Truthfully, he hadn't become Putrid until this past January. He knew a lot about the historical sites in Boston, which I loved, and he made my mom laugh, which was great. Then he started talking about New Hampshire every time I saw him.

"What's so great about New Hampshire?" I asked him, when the Granite State talk was new. That question was a huge mistake. I got swept into a forty-minute lecture about how there was no traffic up there, how beautiful and peaceful it was, and how much space there was. Evidently, he thought Boston—my hometown, my favorite place in the world—was dirty and crowded, and traffic-ridden and awful, and he wanted to leave. Putrid.

What if he wanted to bring Mom and me with him?

"Do-over," Mom said. It's what we say when our conversations start to fall apart or one of us is in a bad mood. Then you change the subject. "New shirt?" she tried.

"Yeah." I tugged on it so Mom could read *The J. Geils Band* scrawled under a white handprint. "I got it from the consignment shop on Centre Street." I collect vintage Boston band T-shirts to go with my typical uniform: a scruffy denim skirt and crazy tights—which, in my opinion, was far less weather-inappropriate than Ms. Leather Boots and Jacket. Today's pattern? Oversize green houndstooth.

"Nice." Mom dresses in suits and very somber outfits for work, but has been known to rock an Aerosmith T-shirt on the weekends. Looks-wise, I'm her carbon copy: same dark wavy hair, round eyes, and wide mouth. We're also super-tiny—a body type most girls I know would kill for.

"Speaking of clothes," I said, "we should probably get me measured for the Uniform of Horror sometime soon."

My mom cocked an eyebrow at me. Although I dreaded wearing the Boston Classics uniform in September, ordering it would be the best test as to Mom and Putrid Richard's intentions. If we were moving to New Hampshire, she wouldn't spend the money on it, right?

"Seriously, Moxie? Can't you wait? You haven't even graduated yet. And what if you change your mind?"

"I'm not going to change my mind," I said. "And you heard what the admissions person said: Smaller sizes need to be ordered in advance. I just think it'd be good to get it out of the way."

Mom sighed and shook her head. Conversation over. Not a good sign.

We pulled into a parking space on Centre Street and entered the restaurant, and just as Mom approached the hostess stand, she did a mini-flail and pocket pat-down.

"I think I left my notebook in the car," she said. She turned to me, apologetic. "I hate not having it. Would you . . . ?"

I sighed and extended my hand for the keys. Even if she wasn't list-making or list-checking, she had to have that paper pile with her.

I jingled the keys in my hand as the door closed behind me, and then, a few steps outside, I stopped short.

Someone was peering into our car.

Someone with long, red, not-streaky hair.

I dropped the keys, frozen. The car was less than a half block away, and there weren't that many people on the street. Adrenaline sizzled my nerves. Had she followed us?

A noisy bus passed, which brought me to my senses. I scooped up the keys, took two giant steps, and crouched behind a mailbox while I tried to catch my breath and slow my heart. Mom would wonder where I was soon, and I needed that notebook or an explanation as to why I didn't have it.

I peeked out from around the mailbox, hoping that the few people on the street thought I was just a kid playing hide-and-seek.

She was gone.

I pulled back to my hiding place.

I tried to think the situation through logically, like this was a math problem: If x, then y.

If she was waiting for me, the only thing she could do was

talk to me. It's not like she could grab me off the street or anything. Right?

If she was hiding and watching, what would she see? Me opening the car door and getting my mom's notebook.

And . . . well, it was *our car*. She was the one spying and being freaky-strange! Why was *I* doing the hiding?

Boldly, I stood and stepped out from behind the mailbox. Ms. Redhead was nowhere to be seen. Once I took the first few steps toward the car, the rest were much easier. No one stopped me, no one yelled boo. I even started to breathe once I hit the passenger door.

It was only when I'd unlocked the car, grabbed the notebook, and slammed the door that I noticed the slip of paper wedged under the passenger-side windshield wiper.

6

Seeing the paper made my skin crawl. I reached out to take it, but paused, hand midair, and scanned the street and buildings to see if someone was watching. Around me, everything looked normal: cars going by, people walking their dogs, waiting for the bus, running into stores.

No redhead in sight.

I tugged the slip out from under the wiper, expecting it to feel electrified or hot or somehow strange, but it was just regular paper. I stuffed it deep in my skirt pocket, dying to read it but also not wanting her to see me do so—why give Ms. Inappropriate Weather Dresser the satisfaction?—and walked two speeds faster than normal back to the restaurant, eyes on the sidewalk.

Opening the door, I glanced into the mirror behind the hostess stand to make sure my face looked okay, not like I'd just been skulking around Centre Street, and prepared myself for the annoying dinner that was to follow. When I found Mom's table, though, I don't think she would have noticed if The Redhead had come in wearing my clothes—her face was a knot of aggravation and she was snapping her patented One-Syllable Angry Responses into her phone:

"Yup." A pause. I slid the notebook over to her.

"Sure." Another pause while she listened. She stuffed the notebook into her purse without even glancing at me.

"Fine." She clicked off the call and slapped the phone onto the table. I knew better than to say anything—speaking to her before she was ready would cause her to redirect her irritation at me. No, thank you.

Finally, she sighed and leaned back in her seat.

"Do-over. We're eating alone," she said. A pause, during which relief poured through me. "Richard has to cover for that idiot Sammy again."

"Okay," I said, not sure why she was so over-the-top about Richard having to work late—she certainly had her fair share of bizarre hours at the funeral home—but happy to have been spared his presence. I was so happy, I almost forgot about the slip of paper in my pocket, which all of a sudden felt like it weighed four pounds.

And once I almost-but-didn't forget about it, I couldn't *not* think about it. A few times I almost went into the bathroom to read it, but I chickened out. What if it said something awful? But, on the other hand, what if we were in danger if I *didn't* read it?

Finally, Mom went to the bathroom. I'd barely touched my burger and fries, and as soon as she turned the corner, I slid my plate away and pulled the slip out of my pocket. For some reason, reading it at the table—in front of all the other people having dinner—felt safer than reading it locked in a bathroom stall.

Surprisingly, the handwriting was bubbly, like those girls' in fifth grade who heart and star their *i*'s. And all that was written was one word:

Liar.

My heart locked up in my chest, and for about two very long seconds I was afraid that it would never start again. I stared at the note.

It wasn't for my mom, that much was clear. The Redhead had totally planted this for me. But what did she think I was lying about? Who was home? Where Grumps was—

Oh.

"*Sweet chocolate bunnies,*" I hissed. I was a complete idiot.

The Redhead had followed me to Alton Rivers.

Mom came back to the table a minute or so later, and by that time I'd stuffed the note into my pocket, was breathing regularly, and was seething mad—at both myself and my annoying psycho stalker—and nearly vibrating with anxiety about Grumps. Was he okay? Should I tell my mom? When Mom asked if I was ready, it took me a second to figure out what she meant.

"Sure," I said. And then . . .

"Hey," I added, "it's still early. Would you mind dropping me off at the Arboretum? Ollie wanted me to meet him." Maybe his parents would still let him out, and hanging with him would help me figure out what to do—and there would be no Mom around, so I could panic in private.

"Okay." She sighed. "But call him now so I know that he'll be there."

I grinned and whipped out my cell, grateful that I'd remembered to bring it. No phone would've been the deal breaker.

"Thanks, Mom."

She left me and my bike at the Water Street entrance and made me promise to be home no later than eight. The Arboretum, or the Arbs, as a lot of people call it, is a huge park just at the edge of our neighborhood. There are all these paths and trees and flowers, and people go there for picnics and festivals and just to hang out. Rumor is that older kids sneak in after dark to party and make out. Based on the number of beer bottles we've seen while looking for caches, I guessed the rumors were true.

For Ollie, the Arbs is like Treasure Island. Geocachers love the park because there are so many cool hiding places.

He was waiting for me at the bottom of Hemlock Hill. I spotted him from the top—short, spiky black hair, gray hoodie, jeans—facing the opposite way, perfect for sneaking up on. I rolled down on my bike as quietly as possible, avoiding rocks and sticks. He never turned around.

When I was about ten feet away, I yelled, "Put your hands in the air!"

Ollie jumped, arms straight over his head. I cracked up, and he turned.

"Gotcha!" I grinned.

"This time. But I'll get you back."

"I'd like to see you try," I teased.

"Just wait," he said. He pulled his portable GPS device from a cargo pocket. "So, according to the coordinates, we should be able to . . ."

I followed him down the hill, locking my bike against one of the gates as we went. Even though I'd asked my mom to drop me off, now that I was here, I wasn't one hundred percent sure I should tell Ollie what was going on. And I wasn't one hundred percent sure this was where I should *be*. Was Grumps okay?

"Mox," Ollie said, and stopped walking. I almost tripped. "What's your deal? Just spill it."

I stared at the ground. There was so much that he didn't know—like who Grumps really was—that I wasn't sure where to start. "This psycho redhead showed up at my door today asking for stuff and making threats and now I'm totally stressed over Grumps's safety" didn't seem like the best opening.

Going for a half-truth, I said, "I'm just worried about Grumps."

"Did something happen?" he said, eyes wide. His only grandparent—his grandmother—lives in Vietnam, so he rarely sees her, and he loves Nini and Grumps like they're his own. He even goes with me to Alton Rivers sometimes.

"No, he's okay," I said quickly. "Just . . . you know . . . the usual." My response sounded lame even to my own ears.

He sighed and pushed his rectangular black-framed glasses

up his nose. "If you aren't going to talk to me about it, that's cool. But your not-Moxie attitude is bringing me down."

"What's that supposed to mean?"

"You've barely said anything, but you're not listening to me. And you were the one who called me to meet up after you said you couldn't. Something else is going on."

Ollie's words triggered both panic and relief in me. Panic, because what if it was as obvious to, say, my mom or Nini that something was bugging me? I'd gotten off easy with dinner because Mom had been distracted over Richard. I didn't know how long I could get away with not being front and center on her radar. Since my dad isn't in the picture—according to Mom, he couldn't handle the truth about Grumps's "lifestyle" and bugged out when I was just a baby, leaving me with his last name and nothing else—I'm the target of Mom's total focus.

The relief, well, that was from someone at least knowing something was wrong. I knew I could trust Ollie with most stuff, but how would he react when he found out that I'd hid a whole other part of my life from him? If you wanted to get specific about it, I'd hidden my *real* life from him. At least, I'd hidden my family's real life. And if that hadn't gone over well with my own father, how would a friend, who totally wasn't related to me, feel about the lie? Besides, was out in the open, where The Redhead might be lurking, the best place to reveal all this info?

Probably not.

"I'm sorry," I whispered. "You're right." Coming here was a bad idea. "But I can't tell you about it."

7

I didn't tell Ollie anything that night even though I knew he was hurt and—let's tell the truth here—probably a little ticked off about the way I'd acted. When I got home from the Arbs, I'd checked my room, stared out the window to see if anyone had followed me home, totally stressed, wondering what The Redhead would do to Grumps (or me) when July 4 rolled around and Sully didn't have what he wanted.

I couldn't calm down at school the next morning either, because every time Wendy Richland passed me in the hall, I'd glimpse her bright red hair (even though hers is a straight bob and totally not the same color as the stalker's) and jump. In second period, Mr. Crespo, my geometry teacher, caught me staring out the window at the parking lot, searching for flashes of red.

"Miss Fleece," he chided as I snapped my head in his direction, "this is the last day of this year. And there are three people in this classroom. Although I'm sure you have big plans for your vacation and beyond, I'd like it if you kept your attention up here."

I flushed and mumbled an apology, then slid down in my

seat. Mr. C. taught advanced math to me and Derek Choi during his free period, and Derek always paid perfect attention. Not that I spaced out all that much; hiding in a room of three people is impossible.

There was no reason that The Redhead would follow me to school. Besides, we had all kinds of security measures to get into the building—adults had to sign in, give their license, practically give blood, as my mother said.

Mr. C. resumed wrapping up geometry, and I relaxed into a world of angles and proofs. Math is consistency. Numbers, angles, equations . . . all of that stuff is solid. Unchanging. No matter what you do—how many plus or minus signs you add, transitive properties you include, or formulas you apply—the numbers are what they are.

Just before the bell, a kid came in with a blue office call slip that he dropped on Mr. C.'s desk.

"Moxie," Mr. Crespo said, "please stop by the front desk on your way to your next class."

So much for being relaxed. My first thought was actually about Grumps. Was he sick? The minutes before the bell seemed like an eternity and my focus was shot.

Class finally ended, and I pushed through the main hall to the front office. Ollie and I shared third-period Cultural Studies (our school's version of social studies), and we usually met at his locker and walked over together. I spotted him, a bulky stack of books in his arms. I grabbed the one on top. It was about China. We'd read it back in October? November?

"I never turned these in," he said, sheepish. I fished one more book out of his locker and took one off his pile, shaking my head at his lack of organization.

"I'll take these, so you don't have to lug all of them. But I got a front office slip, so I'll meet you in class," I said. Before he could ask any questions, I left. I caught him shaking his head as I joined the mess of students in the hall.

Mrs. Clarke, the secretary, was talking to a parent when I came in. I plopped Ollie's books on a chair and hovered at the edge of their conversation, twisting the office slip with both hands, hoping she'd cut off her chatting and tell me what was going on.

"It seems like she started school yesterday," the dad was saying, "and now she's going in to eighth grade. Where does the time go?"

Mrs. Clarke nodded. "It flies," she said, and I caught her eye. "And here's one of our graduates now! Moxie will be leaving us to make room for your daughter's class. Commencement is tomorrow," she informed the dad.

I gave him what I hoped was a "your conversation is over and I need info" smile, and stepped closer to Mrs. Clarke's desk, kind of cutting in front of the dad. Oh well.

"I was called down here?" I showed her my origami'd office slip and the dad retreated.

"Oh, yes, sweetheart. You had a delivery." She shuffled through the papers on her desk and I shifted from foot to foot. "Ready for high school?" she chirped.

A delivery? My palms prickled.

"Uh-huh," I said through clenched teeth. How difficult was it to find a—

"Here it is!" She held out a white envelope, my name in bubbly writing on the front. My body went cold.

Inside was a small piece of paper, and written in that same writing was: *Tell your grandfather hi next time you see him . . . or I will.* My breath hitched. At the bottom was scrawled: *Aunt Sally.*

Very funny.

I leaned against Mrs. Clarke's desk. Other teachers and a few kids had come in during the break, milling around the office, and the noise they made suddenly sounded like it was coming from far away.

No way, I thought. *I will not lose it.* I took a deep breath.

"Are you okay, dear?" Mrs. Clarke said, her face clearly concerned. "Is everything all right?"

I nodded, remembering the way The Redhead looked at me when she said that if Sully didn't get what he wanted, he'd take something of "lesser value." This crazy note-leaving chick was serious.

"Okay then." She was still staring.

I nodded again, and tried to smile. "Thanks, Mrs. Clarke." The third-period bell buzzed, and she scrawled a late slip for me. I paused before I reached the door.

"Um . . . one question," I asked her. "How did this get here? Was it dropped off?" I added, in response to Mrs. Clarke's puzzled expression.

"Oh, yes. A lovely young woman with long red hair brought it in," she answered. I fought the urge to spin around and look for her as though she was still in the office. "Someone you know?"

I nodded, grabbed Ollie's books, and left.

When I got to Cultural Studies, I leaned against the wall next to the door, trying to get it together. My hands tingled with fear. This loony chick was targeting me—*me!*—an eighth grader, for some creepy reason. I mean, sure, I'd been rude to her, but seriously? This was a total overreaction on her part. She was . . . What's that word that they use on cop shows all the time, when the serial killer starts murdering victims even faster . . . ? *Escalating.* She was escalating.

Or whatever Grumps hid for Sully Cupcakes was not "small-time."

Not that that made me feel better. I thought Grumps had been honest with me about his work. Maybe I didn't know him as well as I thought. My eyes prickled and I shook my arms a little to brush off the wave of emotion threatening me. I pushed the thoughts away.

After a few deep breaths, my head no longer felt wrapped in a blanket and my hands stopped trembling. I pushed the door open and went into Cultural Studies. Ollie turned as soon as I came in, a questioning look on his face. I shook my head slightly, left the late slip and Ollie's books on Ms. Beman's desk, and slid into the open seat behind him.

A few minutes later, I tore a strip of notepaper, scribbled "Talk at rehearsal?" on it, and slipped it to him.

Time to come clean.

8

That afternoon before graduation practice, while everyone else raced around getting yearbooks signed, Ollie and I sat at the top of the bleachers in the gym. He was waiting for me to explain what was going on. I fiddled with the record album key chain dangling off my backpack (I'd had to educate a lot of people as to what an album actually *was*, sadly) and directed my eyes anywhere but at him.

"You might get mad at me," I started. Below us, at the bottom of the bleachers, Jolie Pearson and the other Pretties balanced books on their knees and signed them with matching purple and blue sparkly pens. The girls' glittery shininess made me want to yurk, which I took as a good sign—no matter how stressed I was, they were still annoying.

"Why?" Ollie was drawing a map. It went with his geocaching addiction. He hid stuff, drew maps so he'd remember where he put it, and checked to see if anyone found his "treasures"—but he never told anyone what he hid or where. He just tucked random things into odd corners and hoped someone would stumble across them—like the GI Joe action figure that he'd put on the ledge next to a little-used water fountain on the second floor. Took a month for someone to take it. Or the six bouncy balls that he claimed were behind a book on Mr. Crespo's shelf, which Ollie said were still there. He had a ton of random stuff like that stashed all over Henry Knox Junior High. To make sure people didn't confuse his "treasures" with junk, Ollie'd made labels for them. *Congrats!* they read. *Finder's keepers.* There was an icon of an *O* with an *X* through it and his cache handle—Oxnfree—at the bottom.

Although I (frequently) pointed out that the people who found his stuff weren't *looking* for it—they randomly stumbled on it—he didn't care.

Betcha he'd care about this.

"Because I lied to you," I said. "I've been lying for a long time, I guess." I stared at my feet, noting the scuff marks and scars on the wooden bleachers.

Ollie stayed quiet, plotting points of the boys' locker room on his graph paper.

"It's about my family," I began. "It's not—we're not—it's not what you think it is, and I think I'm in trouble because of it. Or not in trouble, maybe, but something's going on."

Jolie Pearson laughed, and everyone in her group giggled, an idiot echo. Ollie slid his pencil into the spiral rings of his notebook, his brown eyes on mine.

"What are you, vampires? Werewolves?"

I couldn't even force a smile.

"No. Not really. But kind of," I said. "We're both bad . . . or, well, I'm not bad. It's Grumps."

"Grumps is in a nursing home, Mox," Ollie pointed out. "What trouble can he get into?"

I shook my head and let go of the key chain, picking at a cuticle instead. "It's not about who he is now, it's what he *was*—a criminal." I felt like I'd dropped a huge weight and, at the same time, picked up another one.

I waited for the gasp, the shock, or for him to turn away. He just watched me.

"And?" he said.

"And what? Aren't you mad?"

"Why would that make me mad?" He shrugged. "There have been rumors around the neighborhood for years that he was shady back in the day. That his restoration job for the city was his front. Didn't you know that?"

"No!" I said, shocked and louder than I'd intended. A few heads turned in our direction and I slouched back against the wall. "No," I tried again, quieter this time but through gritted teeth. How had I *not* known that there were rumors about Grumps in our neighborhood? "I had no idea." I felt sick and betrayed. "Why didn't you ever tell me?"

"You never told me," he pointed out.

"That's different," I snapped. "It was family business. *Private stuff*. I wasn't supposed to say anything to *anyone*."

"Including your best friend, clearly."

Ouch. That stung.

"Yeah, well, *you* should have told *your* best friend that there were rumors around town about my family!" How had I missed so much?

We just sat after that, both of us seething. I watched Jolie Pearson and her group as a million thoughts ran through my mind. A big one: Were the rumors surrounding my family part of the reason why I'd never fit in with other kids in my grade? Had they been avoiding me? It would explain a lot. Not that I'd want to hang out with *that* crew, anyway, I amended.

Ollie finally broke the silence.

"Did he kill anyone?"

"Of course not!" I cried, but at the same time a prickle of doubt entered my mind. Could I be sure? "He'd never do that. He was a carpenter. He hid stuff for people . . . other people," I finished lamely. Seriously, what did I know? Evidently Grumps could've been an assassin and I'd have no idea.

"Other criminals?" Ollie asked.

I nodded.

"Okay," he said. "So what does Grumps's job have to do with what's weirding you out?"

Before I answered, I took a second to think. Grumps was involved with something bigger than I ever knew. Ollie hid stuff from me.

But then I remembered The Redhead, and her message that Sully wanted his items. Soon. And now she knew where Grumps actually was. I needed my best friend—both to help me, and because I trusted him. And even though he hadn't told me about the neighborhood rumors, he'd been (and stayed) my friend in spite of them. So I told Ollie everything about The Redhead, Sully Cupcakes, the note—all of it, ending with the slip I'd gotten this morning.

Ollie whistled through his teeth. Meanwhile, Mr. Crespo and Ms. Beman, our class advisors, called for our attention.

"We'll line up in two lines," Mr. Crespo yelled. "Alphabetical order. Ms. Beman will read your names."

Ollie and I stood and clomped down the bleachers.

"Well," he said when we'd reached the bottom, "I'm not sure about the *best* summer ever, Mox—but it could be the most interesting summer ever."

After rehearsal, Ollie and I walked home together, discussing what to do next. We agreed that telling my mom or Nini would only freak them out, and since the psycho hadn't actually *done* anything but mess with me, worrying them would only get me grounded for my own "safety" . . . and then what would happen to Grumps? Ollie also suggested calling the police, but there was no way I could bring them into it—they could arrest Grumps! My family would never forgive me. I'd never forgive myself.

July 4 was thirteen days away.

"The thing is," said Ollie, "Grumps hid something that Sully wants back. Maybe if we can figure out what he's looking for, we'll know who to tell or what to do. Think of it like a treasure hunt."

I was about to answer when I heard a familiar cackle behind us.

"Going on a date with your geeky *boy*-friend, Moxie?"

Jolie Pearson.

"Nope," I called without even turning around, "I'm on my way to meet *yours*. He likes me way better than you." Then I wrapped my arm across my back and raised a very specific digit.

Next to me, Ollie flushed.

Jolie Pearson likes to think she's some junior high hotshot, but I never take her crap. Seriously, you'd think she'd get tired of throwing insults in my direction, because I always have a comeback for her. My school doesn't have cliques or bullies like you see in the movies—well, except for the Pretties. They like to think they're straight out of Hollywood and try to dress trendy and act mean. They even named *themselves*. Makes me want to gag, or laugh. I'm not sure which.

A frustrated squawking noise came from her direction, and Ollie and I turned to each other and grinned.

But in the back of my mind, I was thinking about what Ollie said—figuring out what the deal was with Sully and Grumps would help me know what to do next.

Or it might get me in a whole lot of trouble.

12 DAYS LEFT

9

I managed to graduate eighth grade without any more random visits from the psychotic redheaded stalker or taunts from Jolie Pearson. One of them, though, was sure to be back.

Graduation was exactly what I expected: Mom and Nini misty eyed, a quiet moment or two when we all missed Grumps at the ceremony (being in large crowds is just too confusing for him, so we planned to bring a cake to Alton Rivers), and a dinner with Putrid Richard, Ollie's mom, dad, and little sister at an awesome restaurant in the North End—the Italian section—of Boston. I picked out special blue zebra-striped tights for the occasion, and even though it was blazing hot, I wore them anyway. They matched my graduation robe. But no matter how excited I was to be done with junior high, I couldn't help keep one eye on the calendar. July 4 was twelve days away, and I hadn't made any progress on the Grumps/Sully Cupcakes puzzle.

As we were getting dessert—tiramisu for me and Ollie, chocolate cake for everyone else—my mom slid a wrapped box across the table.

"What's this?" I asked.

"Your graduation gift," my mom answered. "Open it."

Ollie's mom, who worked in his sister's nursery school, gave me a sneaky grin, then slid the same sized box to Ollie. Mrs. Truong and Mom then sat back, looking very pleased with themselves.

"It's a conspiracy," Ollie said.

"On three?"

He nodded.

"LeeLee, you count," I said to his little sister. She clapped her hands.

"One . . . two . . . five!" she yelled.

We tore the wrapping paper off the boxes, which were plain white, and removed the lids.

"A T pass?!" we said, in unison. What? We'd had subway passes to get back and forth to school since sixth grade. This was not a gift.

The moms burst out laughing.

"We like to think of it as your freedom—within reason," my mom replied.

"As long as you two are together, or you're with someone else from school," Mrs. Truong said, "you can explore downtown on your own this summer."

My mouth opened in shock. Correction: This was the best gift *ever*.

"Don't leave me hanging," Ollie said, nudging me. I gave him a high five without even looking. I'd been to Boston a zillion times, of course, but always with an adult. This was big. *Big.* We could go to the Back Bay and hang out on Newbury Street, ride the Swan Boats in the Public Garden, get ice cream at Faneuil Hall, take the T into Cambridge and go to Harvard Square . . . Ollie could uncover every geocache in the city. I could check out all the vintage record stores I wanted. It really *would* be the Best Summer Ever.

"There are rules," my mother said. She furrowed her brow. "You just can't go off gallivanting all over creation."

"We don't gallivant," said Ollie somberly, which cracked up everyone at the table.

When we stopped laughing, my mom pulled two small cards from—where else—her notebook and handed one to each of us. How had she found them in there?

I glanced at Ollie's; they were both the same. Business-card sized, perfect to slip into a wallet or pocket. On them were printed:

MOXIE AND OLIVER'S RULES, RIGHTS, AND PRIVILEGES
THIS CARD ENTITLES THE BEARER TO:

1. Travel to Boston/Harvard Square with a peer.
2. Spend the summer exploring the city.
3. Return home no later than 9 pm.
   Failure to obey these rules—or traveling without a charged cell phone at all times—will result in immediate suspension of all privileges.

"You are to carry the card with you constantly," Ollie's mom said, "so there are no excuses or negotiating on the rules. Same goes for your cell phones."

Both of us nodded. I jumped up and hugged my mom,

then squeezed Mrs. Truong, Mr. Truong, and LeeLee for good measure. I even gave Putrid Richard a hug.

"And you didn't even tell them the best part," Ollie's dad said.

I looked at Ollie. There was more?

"The cards are preloaded with forty dollars each," Mom answered, smiling.

Score!!

"This might also be of use to you on your adventures," Putrid Richard said. He passed two wrapped packages to us. Inside mine was a guide to Boston's historical sights and Ollie's was a detailed guide to the city's parks and walking trails. Gotta hand it to Putrid Richard, he knows his audience . . . even if he probably *was* plotting to take me away from the place I loved.

I pushed that thought down the turnpike.

"He is so *not* putrid," whispered Ollie. I scowled at him.

Nini also had something for me. She pulled a squat gift bag, bursting with tissue paper, from under the table.

"Grumps wanted me to give this to you tonight instead of tomorrow," she said. It was heavy, and whatever was in it thumped as the bag tilted. I swam through the tissue paper and removed an old brown leather album, the word *Photos* stamped on it in gold lettering.

"See what's in it," she said. Everyone's eyes were on me. Ollie leaned over my shoulder.

I opened the cover and flipped through page after page of photos of Grumps, Nini, and my mom and me. I'd seen lots of them before, but some were of Grumps in different places around Boston—Fenway Park, the old Boston Garden, the state house, the *Constitution.* In those photos, Grumps ranged in age from right before he retired from carpentry, to when he was young and had dark hair. I flipped through slowly.

"Some are from his job sites. He took before and after photos and I thought you'd want those. His work is amazing," she announced proudly. "He made it himself, years ago, and kept updating it. I spruced it up for you."

"Nini, *this* is amazing." My eyes filled with tears. "Thank you."

"Maybe you can go check out some of the work he did around the city this summer," Ollie's dad suggested.

"Totally," I said.

I handed the album to Ollie, then raced around the table. I squeezed Nini so hard that I hoped Grumps felt it too.

10

The next day, at ARC, I gave Grumps a huge hug and thanked him for the photo album.

"You're welcome, Annie," he said, and patted my hand.

"She's not Annie, I am," my mother said. "I'm Anne." Grumps glanced back and forth between the two of us, blue eyes cloudy.

"Don't stress him out, Ma," I whispered. "It's okay."

Mom's knuckles were white as she gripped the cake knife, and her mouth tightened into a line as she sliced. When Grumps was having a bad day, it was best to just go with it, but she didn't get that.

"Do you want some cake, dear?" Nini asked. She tucked a napkin under Grumps's chin and wheeled him closer to the table.

Grumps shook his head. "I don't like cake," he answered.

Mom made a funny hissing sound through her teeth. Grumps—old Grumps, pre-Alzheimer's Grumps—*loved* cake. Like, love-loved it. My heart dropped.

When I visited him on bad memory days, we sat on the porch together and just hung out. Angel told me not to say much when things were rough, just to try and be still and enjoy Grumps's company. It was super-hard—some days more than others—but I'd learned to do it. For me, spending time with him, even if he didn't know I was there, was way more important to me than forcing him to fight the disease that he couldn't beat.

Mom's not big into accepting things.

Nini prattled on about graduation, and I sat next to Grumps, just holding his hand. Mom sliced the cake and put it on small round plastic plates and passed out forks. When we'd finished, Mom and Nini took the leftover cake to the rec room so the staff could share it with the other residents. I stayed with Grumps, who'd started mumbling in his sleep. Now would be the perfect time to push him about Sully Cupcakes, but the thought of sending him into a really bad state scared me.

"Hey, Joe," I said, trying out a deep "tough guy" voice, "it's Sully. Where's my stuff?"

He opened his eyes and stared right into mine.

"I hid 'em, Sully, just like you wanted."

His eyes darted around the room like he wanted to make sure no one was listening, and then he leaned in even closer, whispering even more quietly, "No one will ever find them either."

Ice water ran through my veins, and my vision got a little gray around the edges from my heart slamming so hard. I had to hold it together. Grumps stared at me like he expected a response—his blue eyes were totally focused on mine and his bushy eyebrows nearly met over his nose—and I needed a sec to figure out what the right words would be. How could I get him to tell me more about Sully?

"Where?" I tried.

"Don't ask me *where*," he said harshly, a wavering finger pointing in my direction. His eyes narrowed to slits. Okay, bad tactic. I tried to calm him down.

"I'm not even going to look," I soothed.

Grumps laughed a not-funny laugh. "You'll look, all right," he said, "but you'll never find them. I'm not afraid of you, sweetheart."

Sweetheart? Who does he think he's talking to? I doubted he called Sully Cupcakes "sweetheart."

He put that pointy finger away and folded his hands on the table, right where my cake plate had been.

"I'm sure you hid them really well," I said. I had one eye on the door. Mom and Nini would be back any second, and if they caught me rattling Grumps, I'd be done for.

Grumps nodded. "Sweetie, you have no idea. The concert, especially. So stop asking me, 'cause if you don't, I'll just make a few phone calls and collect the reward money instead." He paused, and I thought he was done. But he pursed his lips together and leaned forward, eyes burning into mine. They were not the soft blue eyes of the grandfather who'd swabbed my cuts and taught me to ride a two-wheeler—instead, they were hard and emotionless. Startled, I had to fight the urge not to push away from the table. Was *this* the real Grumps?!

"I'm not afraid of your two-bit gangster malarkey," he growled. "Don't even *think* of messing with me." After he

52

was done saying that, Grumps flopped back in his seat, tired. Drifting always wears him out, but that one made him extra-tired, because he looked kind of . . . faded, I guess you'd say. He closed his eyes. I closed mine briefly too, in relief.

"I won't," I said.

Grumps responded by snoring softly.

Feeling like I'd just won a scary, twisted lottery, I wiped my sweaty palms on my owl tights and skirt and cleared my throat. A second later, Mom and Nini came back into the room. While Nini tucked a blanket around Grumps, Mom turned a critical eye to me.

"You don't look right," she said. Curse her magical mom-vision!

"I'm fine," I said, probably a little too quickly. Her eyes narrowed.

"I'm going to take him back to his room," Nini said. I lightly pecked Grumps on the head. His fluff of hair tickled my nose.

Mom brushed his hand with hers. "Bye, Dad," she whispered.

The door clicked as they left. I leaned against the wall thinking about Grumps's drift. He'd hid Sully's items, that much was obvious. But who was the "sweetheart" he was talking about? Had The Redhead been to see him? Had she hurt him? Anger boiled in me. I clenched my fists and forced my mind back to what he'd said.

What was up with the concert? Did he hide music? Why would Sully want that?

And what was that bit about the reward money?

11

Later that night, after the silent ride home from Alton Rivers, I found Ollie online and spilled what had happened with Grumps. He didn't know what to make of it either.

Oxnfree: Clock's ticking. What do you think Sully C wants?

HubRockr45: No idea . . . Let's exercise the T pass.

Oxnfree: Totally. Tick-tick-tick.

We decided to head into town around mid-morning. After he signed off to check out cache sites for the trip, I opened my browser history to the block of Sully Cupcakes sites. I clicked the encyclopedia article and read it more carefully this time.

Nothing in Sully's background jumped out at me, so I moved on to the list of crimes. Sully wanted "items" back, and Grumps had said that he'd hid something—actually, he'd said hid "them," which meant more than one thing—but most of the stuff on Sully's list was related to money. Or murder. And I still wanted to believe that Grumps wouldn't do anything as bad as that. I *had* to believe that.

Then, smack in the middle of the article, sticking out like an igloo in a desert, was "1990—Suspected ringleader. Isabella Stewart Gardner Museum Art Theft."

Even though it happened way before I was even born, I knew a little about the Gardner case—everyone in Boston did. At least, everyone who went to public school and took the annual Gardner Museum field trip in sixth grade did. Back in 1990, two guys dressed as Boston cops broke in during the middle of the night and stole a bunch of super-expensive paintings and some ancient artifacts, and they'd never been caught. And the stuff has never turned up. But here's the creeptastic part of the whole story: Because of the agreement that Isabella Gardner, the founder of the museum, had set up ages ago, *the museum has to leave the stolen paintings' empty frames hanging on the wall.*

I shuddered, remembering walking into the gallery and seeing the blank outlines. The spots make you feel both sad and guilty—sad because they're a reminder that you'll never see what's supposed to be there, and guilty because it's like those empty rectangles accuse everyone who walks in of hiding the missing art.

There was a link to the encyclopedia entry about the Gardner situation, and I clicked over to that. It outlined the basics of the theft—thirteen pieces stolen in one night, including eleven paintings, a ku (which is a museum-fancy word for *vase*), and an eagle doohickey off the top of an old flagpole. A five-million-dollar reward was offered for their return. Five million! Then there was a list of the names of the paintings, with a little image of each one. I scrolled down, and there, in bright blue letters, I saw:

Vermeer, *The Concert* (1658–1660).

The painting was of three people: a long-haired man, whose back was to the viewer, and two women. One had pigtails and was playing a piano-looking instrument, and the other was singing. The floor was a black-and-white checkerboard pattern, and the people were way at the back of the painting, with some other instruments closer to the front.

Earlier, when he'd mentioned "the concert," I thought Grumps was talking about music, but seeing the title of the painting set off a chain reaction in my brain:

Grumps hid stuff. Really well, evidently.

The Gardner art was still missing.

Grumps hid stuff for Sully Cupcakes.

Grumps mentioned "the concert."

There may as well have been a flashing neon EQUALS sign in my bedroom, it was so obvious:

Grumps had hidden the art for Sully Cupcakes, and now that Sully was out of prison, he wanted it back. That's what The Redhead was sent to get!

And I realized that I had a very big problem. There was no way for Sully to get the art back, unless Grumps remembered where he'd put it. And based on the conversation I'd had with him at Alton Rivers, even if he *did* still know where it was, he had no plans to tell Sully. Why didn't he want Sully to have the art (besides the obvious—that it was stolen and belonged in its museum)?

Regardless of Grumps's motives in keeping the paintings a secret, this was *not* "small-time" work. My hands tingled and my knees went watery. In math, no matter how many times you do a problem, there's only one right answer. Every way I looked at the evidence in front of me, Grumps's involvement in the Gardner heist was the only conclusion. And that was not the answer I wanted.

I counted the squares on my calendar: Eleven days to find out the truth before something awful happened. And, despite all of the doubts I had about Grumps, I was totally certain about one thing: Sully Cupcakes was not messing around. That threat from The Redhead was real. Who should I tell?

What would I do, go into some police station and say: "My Alzheimer's-suffering criminal grandfather probably hid the paintings from the Gardner museum for Sully Cupcakes, but I don't know where or when. Oh, and now Sully wants them back or he's going to do something awful to me. Maybe." That was crazy! No one would believe me. My mom and grandmother would probably kill me for going to the police and breaking family trust, and Grumps—no matter what state he was in—would be furious. I knew that much. Besides, even if I *didn't* go to the police, and told Mom instead, she would totally flip over my safety. Before I could climb the flight of stairs to my room, my stuff would be packed and headed to the Granite State. And who knows if Nini would even be able to get Grumps into a facility as good as Alton Rivers up there? Maybe they'd have to stay behind, and Sully would be after them!

Better something happen to me than one of them. I was on my own.

I needed a plan of attack, some logical steps to follow to

make sure I did the right thing. I sat at my desk, doodling in a notebook as I thought it through. What if the paintings were found? What if Grumps's hiding place was revealed? Sully would go away, we'd be safe, no spontaneous move to New Hampshire, problem solved.

I started to get that nagging "missing piece to a math problem" feeling . . .

It came to me like a flash as I was shading a question mark. Duh! I was staring at my geometry notebook! The most reasonable of all math. Mr. Crespo had said that we could use geometry proofs to perfectly reason out any puzzle—from what to have for dinner to what movie to see. If I could literally do a proof on the Gardner situation, maybe I'd be able to figure out where Grumps put the paintings!

I flipped to a blank page and drew a giant T. Across the top of the sheet I wrote the statement, which is what the proof is trying to, well, prove. I whack-whack-whacked the table with the pencil, and then printed: *Grumps hid the paintings from the Isabella Stewart Gardner Museum art theft for Sully Cupcakes.* Seeing the words on the page caused my breath to lock up in my chest, but I kept going.

Underneath the statement came the given, which is what you know so far about the problem you're about to solve. *Grumps said that he'd hid "them" from Sully, which he'd never find—especially* The Concert—*and now there's a psycho redhead stalking me and trying to get the art back*, I wrote. I paused, then added, *By the Fourth of July.*

Eleven days.

Below those lines was the proof box: that big letter *T*. On the left side, above the cross line, I wrote *Statements*. On the right were *Reasons*. At the very bottom of the statements column, I re-printed the initial statement. Now I just had to go through the steps of filling out the proof: Each time I found out a fact, I'd write it in the statements column. And then I'd give the reason in the reason column. It'd create a step-by-step path right to the truth—or, in this case—the paintings.

I dropped my pencil on the desk, leaned back in my chair, took a deep breath, and surveyed myself. No jitters, no pounding heart. Setting up the proof had calmed me down and now, at least, I had a place to keep my thoughts. The next thing I needed to do was identify the steps needed to solve the problem.

Step one: a visit to the Isabella Stewart Gardner Museum.

12

Ollie frowned and turned away from me as the T bumped its way into Boston. I leaned my head against the probably-filthy window behind me, not caring that gnarly bacteria were setting up shop in my follicles.

"Seriously, Moxie? C'mon. This is a timed cache. Can't we go to the museum after?" He cocked his head at me and I clamped my lips shut. Ollie wanted to head straight into Back Bay so we could go to the Public Garden and search for a cache.

"The cache is part of a contest," he explained patiently, like he was talking to his three-year-old sister. "And how fast you find it determines the number of points you get."

"Points toward what?"

"The next level."

"You are *not* serious," I said. "It's an imaginary game! I'm talking real-life stuff here." I rubbed my face. I needed to start this proof like a wolf needs to howl. Ollie would come around.

He thumped his head against the window and stuffed his hands in the pockets of his cargo shorts and glared at me out from under the brim of his Sox hat.

"Fine," he snapped. "But we go from there straight to the Public Garden."

Victory!! To show him how serious I was, I crossed my eyes and my heart. "Absolutely," I said, trying not to grin or anything.

The train let us out downtown. It was gorgeous outside, but already hot at barely ten—and we decided to walk over to the Gardner instead of switching trains. A couple of blocks into our walk, he wiped his forehead.

I barely noticed the climbing temperature. Although I didn't know what to expect at the museum, the closer we got, the more my heart pounded. It was like the sidewalk was electrified: I bounced up to balance on a low wall in front of Simmons College, then swung around a light pole.

"You are such a dork," Ollie said.

"I totally am," I said, and did a little skip-hop over a tree root in the sidewalk. "But I seriously think that I'm gonna find something today."

"What did you lose, little girl?" The voice came from behind me, and I stopped short, nearly tripping. My spine froze.

Ollie's head snapped around and he stopped walking too. I didn't even have to look. I knew who it was.

"Can I help you find it? See, I've lost something too." Her buttery voice dripped contempt again.

I wanted to book it out of there, but what good would that do? Instead, I turned around slowly and casually, faking it, like I didn't care she was right behind me. Like I didn't care that she was following me around the city. Like I didn't care that she was as unpredictable as a scorpion.

She was leaning against one of the college's gates, inspecting the navy polish on her fingernails and dressed all in black again, like she didn't care how hot it was. Her eyes flicked from her hand to my face in a lazy way, like she was pretending she didn't care I was there. Only in this case, I was *supposed* to know that she was pretending. I clamped my lips together. Out of the corner of my eye, Ollie's head swiveled in all directions. What was he looking for, help?

As if.

After waiting one more beat, I titled my head toward her. "You couldn't help me find my butt with two hands and a flashlight," I said pleasantly, as if I were speaking to Jolie Pearson and not some psycho gangster lady.

Her mouth went into a tight line. Next to me, Ollie chuckled. I wanted to grin, but I kept my eyes on The Redhead, expression steady. Kept pretending that I knew what I was doing.

"Classy," she snarled. "Bet your grandfather would be proud to hear that come out of your mouth."

"You don't know *anything* about my grandfather!" I shouted, instantly so mad, I saw purple, and then, even before the slow smile appeared on her face, I realized the mistake I'd made, letting her get to me. Idiotville: Population—Moxie.

"Enjoy your educational experience at the museum," she purred, obnoxious smirk on her face. "Hopefully it will help you trigger your grandfather's memory so he can tell me where Sully's items are."

"So it *is* the art you want," I said, triumphant. Two could play the "get under your skin" game. "Thanks for confirming."

"Of course that's what it is, genius. And Sully will do whatever it takes to get his hands on it. Or is that 'take whatever he wants' to get his hands on it?" She cocked an eyebrow at me. "Maybe I should spend some time with your mommy or grammy, and see if they can help me find them?" She pushed off from the gate.

Mom and Nini? I couldn't let them get involved in this. What if they got hurt? They were all I had.

"Don't you go *near* them," I growled, forcing strength into my voice that I didn't feel. "I'll get the paintings for you. Promise."

The Redhead gave me a slow, predatory smile, and headed down the street in the opposite direction. After a few long steps she turned and waggled her fingers at me. "Do it. You have ten days, sweetheart."

I turned to Ollie, who was pale, but had a determined expression on his face.

"Psycho," he whispered. "Forget the Public Gardens, Mox. We've got work to do."

A few minutes later we were inside the cool darkness of the Isabella Stewart Gardner Museum. The bored desk guy handed us a map and barely looked at us, but the lady checking our ticket at the door raised a skeptical eyebrow.

"We don't like unaccompanied minors touring the exhibits alone," she said.

"What? Do you think we're going to tag the walls?" I snapped, still annoyed from losing my cool with The Redhead and rattled about the promise I'd made.

Her face turned an ugly brick color and she puffed up like a plump pillow. Ollie stepped forward and put his hands out before she could say anything.

"We're very responsible, ma'am, and just want to look at the art."

Her face was still that brick color, but she deflated. Ollie has that effect on grown-ups—not that they deflate around him, but they trust him. Maybe it's the glasses?

Whatever it was, it worked. She stepped back, took our tickets, and let us in.

I'd been to the Gardner in sixth grade, but hadn't really remembered much about it except for the empty frames. What we stepped into wasn't a dark and dusty museum, but instead an open and airy indoor . . .

"Courtyard," said Ollie. Who, of course, was staring at the map. "We should be in the courtyard." I nudged him with an elbow and he looked up.

"Whoa."

The courtyard was this big rectangular space with stone columns and arches all around it. Flowers and plants grew in this crazy riot of color, and a fountain splashed and trickled. A statue of a woman wearing one of those toga things with her hair up in a pile on her head stood off to one side. It looked like she was reaching for something, only she had no arms.

Why are there so many sculptures of armless women?

I took a deep breath of fresh flower-smell, and next to me, Ollie sneezed.

Even though I wanted to get up to where the not-paintings were, the courtyard was so beautiful we had to walk around it. It's roped off, so you can't go all the way in, but there are cool window-benches all the way around that are close to the plants.

"This is the perfect place to set up a mad cache," Ollie said as we stood in front of a giant planter box bursting with ferns and huge white flowers. He sniffled. I dug a tissue out of my pocket and passed it to him. His eyes watered a little.

"Taking a wild guess, but I bet caching here is totally out of the question," I said. "They've, ya know, probably had enough with people taking stuff out of the museum."

Now it was Ollie who turned brick red.

"Oh. Yeah," he said. "You're probably right about that." He blew his nose into the linty tissue.

"Dutch Room?" I asked. Ollie nodded and sneezed again.

"Sweet. Let's find some paintings."

13

"This is like how Nana's parlor used to be," whispered Ollie.

"If Nana collected real art instead of those doofy Thomas whoever paintings." Ollie's grandma on his mom's side lived in a big old house near Salem before she died. She was the type of grandma who didn't want you to touch anything because she was afraid it might get dirty. There were plastic covers on her couch and rug.

Ollie raised an eyebrow. "He *was* the painter of light, Moxie," he said in his Very Serious Voice. I tried not to crack up. A security guard sitting in a chair glanced in our direction. The museum had only opened a short time ago, and we had the room to ourselves.

The Dutch Room is big and rectangular, and everything in it oozes richness—not rich like money-rich, but rich like thick and beautiful richness. Two of the empty frames were across from where we walked in: big, golden squares that showed only wallpaper and tiny shreds of canvas from where the paintings were cut out. Ollie and I gasped as we stood in front of them.

Tiny plaques with the names of the paintings—Rembrandt's *Storm on the Sea of Galilee* and *A Lady and Gentleman in Black* still hung on the wall, lonely.

"Creepy, isn't it?" The security guard had come up behind us. He scratched at his almost-white mustache. "There's another empty frame." He pointed to a table near the door. It was where *The Concert* had stood. We'd walked right past it. The big blank spots on the wall had grabbed our attention first.

I nodded.

He launched into a long story about the theft—stuff that Ollie and I both knew, but we listened anyway. Well, I listened. Ollie shifted and ran his eyes over every nook and cranny in the room. He'd walk out with it memorized.

"Yep," finished the guard. He hitched his pants up around his waist. "They don't have any idea who took the stuff." He paused, then leaned in close. Too close—I got a whiff of breakfast sausage and maple syrup. "But I think I know what happened to it."

My ears perked up like a cat hearing a can opener. Ollie's attention changed too. I didn't want to appear too overexcited, though, so I cocked my head and tried to act casual.

"Yeah?"

The guard nodded.

"I think they're hanging in some collector's room," he said. More maple syrup/sausage air in my face. "Some wicked rich art collector has 'em." Only when he said it, in his thick Boston accent, *art* came out like *ahht*.

My heart, which had started to beat heavier in my chest, slowed down.

"Oh," said Ollie, voice as disappointed as I felt. This guy had no idea what he was talking about.

"Um, yeah. Well . . . I hope they find the paintings someday," I said. Time to leave Officer Breakfast.

According to the flyer I'd printed off the website, there were six paintings, a small etching, and a little vase stolen out of the Dutch Room. Ollie and I did a quick walk-through and looked at the other empty frames. The little etching wasn't actually in a frame, just under glass on the wall. The wall was still scratched up from where the thieves pried it off. The ku had been on the table under *The Concert*.

"It was small enough to stick in a cargo pocket." Ollie sketched its location on the flyer and showed me the image: It looked like a little beaker, nothing special . . . just thousands of years old.

My head swam. The Redhead had confirmed what I suspected when we were outside: Grumps had hid the Gardner art. Could I get him to tell me where it was? And then there was the nagging voice in the back of my mind—paired with a sickening sensation in my stomach. I turned to Ollie.

"How *could* Grumps have hid the paintings? They were so beautiful, and there's *only one of each of them in the world.* Everyone should be able to see them," I whispered. "Besides, if Sully Cupcakes had been in prison all this time, unable to hurt him, *why hadn't Grumps returned them?*"

Ollie gave me a sympathetic look. "I don't know, Mox. I'm

sorry. Maybe we'll know when we figure out where they are."

I sighed. With the way Grumps was slipping, I didn't know if I'd ever get answers.

We crossed the hall, went through two other rooms, and entered the Short Gallery. Here, some of the art was hung on a rack of window-sized hinged panels—kind of like how doors are hung at big hardware stores.

"You can display a bunch of small pieces of art this way," Ollie said. He flipped a panel open. Five small Degas sketches were taken out of there. Five empty spots, each about the size of a sheet of paper, labeled with the date of the theft, were all that was left of them.

"Up there." Ollie nudged me and pointed next to the door, where an old, stained flag was covered by heavy glass. I wasn't sure what I was supposed to be looking at.

"The top of the flagpole," Ollie whispered. The room was nearly empty, but being around the art made us talk like we were in a library.

The top of the flagpole was . . . the top of the flagpole. "Huh?"

"They took an eagle statue off it." Ollie showed me the picture in his pamphlet.

"Oh." That made five paintings and the ku stolen from the Dutch Room, and five sketches and one doohickey stolen from the Short Gallery. Did the numbers mean anything?

"Kinda weird, huh?" Ollie creased the printed theft list in his hands.

"What do you mean?"

"Five paintings from each room, plus one artifact"—of course Ollie knew the word right away—"from each." I needed to get some of this stuff on paper.

"Totally." I nudged him and pointed through the door under the flagpole. It opened into a room with a ton of chairs set in rows for sitting and looking at the art. Ollie followed me.

"This is the Tapestry Room," he said.

It was kind of an obvious name, if you ask me. Giant rug-like tapestries, woven with pictures of knights and unicorns and stuff, hung from the walls. The room was cool and dark. We crashed into chairs at the back, and I unfolded the proof sheet from my back pocket and smoothed it on the chair next to me.

"Is that a *math* problem?" Ollie said. He cocked his head at me.

"Kind of," I muttered. "It was the only way I could make sense of this stuff."

Did I have anything new to add? Seeing the place where the art was stolen helped me understand what was taken, but looking at the proof, none of that seemed relevant.

"At least we know how big everything was," Ollie said.

"Oh. Yeah! I totally didn't think of that," I responded. The paintings from the Dutch room were big—poster-sized.

"The landscape one was even painted on wood." He unfolded the printout again. "And that was big. I wonder if it was heavy?"

"Probably. And anyway, it's not like they could have

70

stacked everything up and carried it out in one trip," I added. "They must have made two trips to carry all of it." That was something I could put on my proof!

Ollie was flipping through my Boston guidebook, looking for more info on Isabella.

"It says here that she hated change, Moxie, and that she designed the house specifically for her pieces and that's why she never wanted anything moved. She also was well-known around Boston because she wouldn't take crap from anyone. People said she used to walk lions down Boylston Street!"

I grunted a response, too busy thinking about the art.

Ollie nudged me. "Sound familiar?"

"Huh?" I turned to him, surprised.

"Let's just say I think you and Isabella would have gotten along really well," he said, a mischievous grin on his face.

I considered what he was saying. I could definitely identify with what Isabella was doing when she set up the museum; and . . . okay . . . maybe Ollie had a point. Neither of us cared about what other people thought of us.

Isabella and I could have been buddies, maybe, and that made finding the art even more personal.

I pulled a pencil out of my back pocket and scrawled *Art was removed in two trips* in the statements column. Across from it, under reasons, I added *Size of paintings, number of objects stolen.*

"So what happens when you get that whole thing filled out—assuming we can do that in ten days?" he asked, surfacing from his reading.

I refolded the paper and stuck it in my pocket. "Well, in *theory*, I'll know where the paintings are. And then we'll magically find them!"

I laughed, but we had no choice but to try. Because if I didn't, The Redhead would go after Nini. Or my mom. Or I'd end up living in New Hampshire. I shivered.

"We *do* have an advantage that no one else has," Ollie said after a minute.

"What's that?" I answered, preoccupied with the notion of life in the woods with Putrid Richard and his mustache.

"We know who hid them."

14

Our walk to the pizza place over by Fenway Park wasn't as bouncy or thrill-filled as our trip to the museum. Between the creepy redhead popping up, and seeing the voids left in the museum, I was definitely *not* swinging around light poles. More like trudging through syrup.

"This is serious stuff," said Ollie quietly. It was the first time either of us had spoken since we left. I grabbed two goopy, cheesy slices of pizza from the guy at the counter and Ollie followed me to a booth.

"No kidding." Hot cheese burned the roof of my mouth. I chugged from my iced tea bottle and hoped my throat wouldn't melt.

"Like, really serious." He pushed his glasses up on his nose. Taking a hint from my scalding experience, Ollie sat and let his slices cool. "Like . . . I dunno, Moxie . . ."

There was a slight catch—a splinter, almost—to his voice. My insides jell-ified. Ollie could *not* bail on me! I narrowed my eyes and leaned over our lunch, catching a delicious nose full of garlic, cheese, and tomato sauce. The aroma didn't quite fit the mood, but whatever.

"You can *not* back out of this, Ollie. Seriously! My family is in danger. *I'm* in danger!"

"Uh . . . Mox? That's why I think it's a good idea to back out. What if you—*we*—get hurt?" He picked at the edge of his napkin, not meeting my eyes.

I slumped in my chair. "I know. This is big-time stuff. But The Redhead hasn't actually *done* anything to hurt me"—*yet*, I wanted to add, but didn't—"and if I can find the stuff, everything will be totally fine. They'll leave me alone." Even as I said the words, a splinter of my own doubt crept in. Would they *really* leave me alone? "Besides, what else can I do? You heard what she said about my mom and grandmother this morning."

The question hung there. I was daring Ollie to say the words, and he knew it. He blew out a puff of air and stared me straight in the eyes.

"Go to the police."

I snorted. "Yeah, right. Tell the police that my grandfather— my Alzheimer's-suffering, nursing-home-bound grandfather— hid the Gardner art." I lowered my voice for that last part. "As if. They'd arrest Grumps! It would destroy my family."

Ollie shifted and tugged his Sox cap lower. He loved Grumps, and my family . . . right? He wouldn't want to see them pulled into a big mess . . . right?

"It's just . . ."

I waited. He squirmed, and said something so low, I could barely hear. Our pizza slices had gone from steaming to soggy.

"What?" He fidgeted for a minute, and then . . .

"I'm scared," he whispered.

Oh.

"Me too," I said. I hadn't even really realized it until Ollie said it, but it was true. This was scary. Mega-scary. But I had no choice. Scared or not, I had to find the art. "But I have to do this. If you're too scared to help me out, that's okay." The words were a total lie, and I forced them out like bad-tasting berries, but what could I do? It's not like I could demand that he help me and put himself in the way of The Redhead.

He looked out the window. I followed his gaze. People were going by, having a normal summer day. There was a tourist family sitting at a table near us (you could tell because they were completely decked out in Boston gear—Sox T-shirts and hats, and the mom was carrying one of those canvas bags with a lobster and *Cape Cod* stenciled on it), and they were all enjoying their lunches like they had nothing to worry about except grease stains.

Ollie sighed. "I'll stick around," he said. "But if this gets out of control, you have to promise that we'll get help."

I promised him, but as I spoke the words, I knew that if things got out of control, we'd be in no position to help ourselves, let alone *get* help.

After scarfing our cold pizza, Ollie and I headed to the Public Garden for that timed cache as a way to chill. As he pulled his yellow portable GPS out of his shorts pocket and started entering coordinates, his shoulders dropped away from his ears and his tight expression smoothed.

"It's this way," called Ollie, taking off over the footbridge. I followed slower, watching the Swan Boats slip in and out of the barred shadow cast by the bridge. Crazy-cool bright orange and red flowers framed both sides of the path. I focused on them, and breathing. I had to clear my head so I could think.

Across the bridge, Ollie was scrabbling at the bottom of a huge tree near the *Make Way for Ducklings* statue. A flock of little kids were perched on the backs of the ducks, moms and dads clicking away on their cameras. The families seemed so normal on the outside; what secrets were *they* hiding?

I shook my head, clearing the creepy thought, then followed the path past the ducklings and around a bend.

"Boo!" came a voice right behind me.

I jumped, then turned and swatted at Ollie.

"Just getting you back from that night in the Arbs," he said. His face was flushed and sweaty, like he'd been running, but his grin was wide.

"You found it?"

His grin got wider, if that was possible. It made his glasses ride up on his cheeks. He held out a closed fist. "Olly-olly-oxen-free!" he cheered. We high-fived.

"Wait'll you see what was in the box," he added. He turned his hand over and opened it.

"That's it?"

In his palm was one of those green plastic army guys that kids play with. You know—they wear helmets and have that flat piece that connects their feet?

Ollie shook his head like I didn't have 600 other life-or-death-or-art things on my mind.

"I know this guy! Well, not in real life," he amended. "He's GI Goh—one of the best cachers in the city. And he only leaves one army guy in each cache. It means I got here first."

"Nice!" I high-fived him again. "You are so good at this."

"I like hunting for stuff. Why're you over here?" he said. He patted the army guy, then tucked him into the cargo pocket with the GPS and buttoned the flap.

I shrugged. "Just thinking and walking."

"Back to our real-life treasure hunt, huh?" he said. "I wish he'd left coordinates somewhere, like in a geocache."

"That'd be so easy!" I laughed at the thought of Grumps plotting his hiding places on graph paper, like one of Ollie's drawings.

"Well," he said, "it's not a crazy idea. I mean, he had to keep track of things somehow, right?"

"Probably." I sighed and plopped down on a nearby bench. "I just don't know what to do next to figure it out," I said.

Okay, I whined.

Tick-tick-tick . . .

"Bust out that math problem," Ollie suggested. "Can't hurt."

Good point. I tugged the proof out of my back pocket. *Think logically, Moxie.*

"We've established that a lot of the art was big, probably heavy, and they'd have to take it out of the museum in two trips," I said.

"The thieves would have had to meet Grumps to give him the stuff," Ollie added helpfully. "Unless you think they brought it to your house or whatever?"

"No way. Grumps wouldn't bring anything like that to our house. Too dangerous." At least, that's what the Grumps I *thought* I knew would do. But seriously, did I have any idea? I filed that away. We *did* have an awful lot of closets in our house . . .

"So he would've met them somewhere," said Ollie. "And once he saw the art . . ."

My brain was finally in gear. "He'd see what he was dealing with and have to figure out where to hide all of it." I scribbled *Size of pieces determine hiding places* in the statements column, and under reasons, added *Many sizes, shapes, and materials to consider.*

"By the next morning, everyone in the city was looking for it," I mused. "Depending on when the thieves called Grumps—right after the robbery, or the next day—he wouldn't have much time to plan."

"Unless he was in on it from the beginning, and already worked out the hiding places."

"If that's the case, we'll *never* find them," I said. "They could be anywhere in New England." I groaned.

"Wait, though. That can't be right," said Ollie.

"Why not?"

"Think about it: If Grumps had time to plan where he was going to put the pieces, chances are he'd have to run the hiding places by Sully Cupcakes—or whoever was in charge—

78

first. And we wouldn't be here. My guess is that they freaked out at the reaction that the theft caused, and panicked . . ."

"And then they went to Grumps!" We slapped hands. "I'm pickin' up what you're laying down, Ols."

Under statements: *Thieves panicked, went to Grumps to hide art.* Reasons: *Surprised by intense reaction; don't know where paintings are.*

"So Grumps probably wouldn't have had a lot of time to figure out good hiding places," I said. My hands were sweating, heart racing. We were so totally onto something!

"And he would've picked places he was already familiar with!" Both of us said it at the same time, and—I'll admit it—I squealed like Jolie Pearson when she sees a *darling* accessory.

I couldn't sit down anymore. I paced in front of the bench. "So now it's just a matter of narrowing down the right places," I said. A gaggle of moms pushed squeaky strollers past us.

"Which is kind of what we've had to do from the beginning," Ollie pointed out. "We need a list of the places in town where he worked."

I was about to scowl at him, but then it hit me:

"We might have everything we need right in our hands!" I exclaimed. I spun, ready to race to the T, and barely heard his startled "Huh?"

"The list!" I tossed over my shoulder. "It's the photo album!"

Ollie pounded the pavement behind me.

15

We didn't let up our speed until we were back in my bedroom, photo album in our hands. I clicked on a Boston tunes playlist, and The Dropkick Murphys' "Shippin' Up to Boston" filled the room.

"I'm shippin' up to Bos-ton . . . to find my wooden leg!" we both shouted. I laughed my first real laugh in a while. Aside from the family in danger/being threatened by a psychotic redhead thing, being a quasi-detective was *fun*.

We sat on the floor, backs against my bed, and flipped the pages. Shots of Grumps, eyes crinkled, hair kaleidescoping from salt and pepper to all salt and back again, holding a hammer in almost every one, dashed by: in front of the USS *Constitution*, in a pew in a church, standing in front of Paul Revere's house—it was like a historical tour of the city.

"How do we know when he was working on what?" Ollie asked as my flipping became more frantic.

I slowed turning the pages. "Good question."

Ollie carefully peeled back the plasticky coating on the pics and pulled out a photo of Grumps in front of Faneuil Hall. It came off the gluey paper with a slight kissing sound.

"Bà dates the back of all the pictures she sends from Vietnam," he said in response to my cocked eyebrow. He turned the photo over.

Written in Nini's black, spidery writing: 6/94. No matter where they're from, I guess grandmas are alike.

"Disco," I whispered. In that second a zillion feelings raced through me: total happiness, excitement, and—okay, I admit it—fear. Add gratefulness to Ollie's Vietnamese grandmother to that list too.

I grabbed a pen and pile of sticky notes off my desk.

"What're those for?" Ollie asked. He peeked at the back of a different picture and returned it.

"So I can mark what picture goes where when we find the right ones," I explained. Even though part of me was dying to just rip everything out and toss it onto the floor, the other— more rational—part remembered how important this album was to me, Nini, and Grumps. I couldn't just tear it apart.

Ollie and I went through each page (of course, the photos weren't in date order), peeling off the pictures, checking the back, and re-sticking them in the book.

Halfway through the album, none of them matched the date we needed.

"Maybe there aren't any in here from 1990," I said. "I mean, wouldn't it be kind of dangerous to have a record of where the pieces could be?"

Ollie shrugged. "Could be. But wouldn't that *also* tell us something?"

Yeah, I wanted to say—it would tell us that finding the

missing art was going to be way harder than we thought. But I kept that to myself.

My butt was numb. Ollie turned a page and I tugged on a shot of Grumps standing in front of an apartment building somewhere. Half expecting another dead end, I flipped it over and saw *2/90* in Nini's scrawl.

Numb butt forgotten, I popped off the floor and rocked out a twirl.

"Yeah, baby!" Ollie cheered.

I didn't even care that the picture was taken *before* the Gardner heist—photos from the right year existed!

Three pages later, we had it: a shot of Grumps, standing on the stairs in front of a brick building. Squinting into the camera, he had one foot propped a step above him, hands in his pockets. And there, on the back: *3/90*. My heart thudded.

"This could be it," I whispered. Ollie nodded.

"Where is it?" Ollie said. We both stared at the photo: concrete stairs, a black iron gate, blurry bricks in the background. "It looks familiar . . ."

I raced to my computer, scanned the photo, and uploaded it for a Google Image search. The search wheel spun and spun . . . then . . . "Look!"

Best guess for this image: the Massachusetts State House.

Set back on a hill, behind a big iron fence, the state house manages to be both welcoming—it does kind of look like a giant house, with big columns and normal-sized doors and whatever—and intimidating, like the person who lives there would never let you in. The trim around all the doors and windows is white, the actual building is red, and there's a gold-covered dome that shines like the sun on top. During World War II, they painted the dome black so it wouldn't be a target for the Germans (seriously, Massachusetts public education teaches you the most random historical facts ever).

"Same stairs and gate," Ollie said, looking back and forth between the two images.

"And look at the arches," I added. He nodded.

"It's the state house," he said.

I scrawled *state house stairs* on a sticky note and we placed it in the blank album spot. As I did, a chill ran down my spine: The space in the middle of the other photos reminded me of the empty frames left behind at the Gardner.

I shook it off and dug through my desk for an empty envelope. I took another look at the photo, where the not-lines were on Grumps's face, and tucked it away.

"Could he really have gotten all that art into *that* building?" Ollie said. He'd closed the album and laid it across his knees. "I mean, we're talking about where the governor works. And all kinds of officials. And security guards. That's gutsy."

Still standing, I stretched my cramped legs. "Yeah, but it kind of makes sense," I said, thinking it through as I spoke. "I mean, he'd have tools and stuff that he'd have to carry in, right?"

"Yeah."

"Well, what if he was able to disguise the art like it was

part of his gear? If the stuff *is* actually in there, it's not like he hung it on someone's office wall or anything. It's been hidden for over twenty years."

"True," Ollie confirmed. "Now we just have to figure out where in the building it is. And," he added, "it might not even all be there, if he was working on more than one place at a time. I still think it's worth it to check the house too."

Before I could agree with him, there was a knock at my bedroom door. I nearly jumped out of my skin.

"Moxie!" called my mom. "Hey!"

"Just a sec!" I called back. I grabbed the album, shut and stuffed it back into the bag next to my bed. Then I raced to the door, a jittery ball of nerves. I didn't dare look at Ollie.

"Hey," I said, opening the door. "I didn't hear you come in."

"Not over the music," she said. She was still wearing her work clothes, which meant she hadn't been home for very long. Where had the day gone? Her eyes skipped behind me, to Ollie. Immediately my face flushed.

"Hey, Ollie," she said. Eyes back to me, narrowed in the Death Glare.

Technically, I was not supposed to have anyone over when my mom was at work. Not even Ollie, unless we were hanging out in Nini's apartment.

Another family rule.

"Er, hi," Ollie said. His face was as red as mine felt. I'm sure my mom took our joint humiliation explosion as acknowledging that we'd broken the rules, not that we were hiding the potential solution to a decades-old, multi-million-dollar mystery.

Mom stuck her hands on her hips.

"Ollie, it's time for you to head home," she said.

"Uh-huh," he muttered. He scrabbled for his hat, patted his pockets to make sure he had everything, and squeezed past me. "Later, Mox," he said.

My mom still blocked the door, her five-foot-nothingness seeming to fill the whole space. "You and Moxie know the rules, Ollie," she said with a deadly calm. I watched the back of his head bob up and down. Mom was scarier than The Redhead, for sure.

"I'm sorry, ma'am," Ollie said. Ollie was polite to adults, but he only busted out the *ma'am* when it was serious business—like now. "It won't happen again."

"Damn straight," Mom said. She shifted to the side, allowing him to pass, and shifted her gaze to me. He pounded down the stairs. I heard the apartment door click closed behind him.

"You didn't have to scare him to death," I said. I'd regained control of my jumpy nerves. "We weren't up here that long." My mom knows Ollie and I are just friends—the idea of kissing him would be like kissing my cousin. Or brother—but she short-circuits sometimes.

"I don't care *how* long you were up here," my mom snapped. "You know he's not supposed to be up here. At. All." She clipped those last two words. "Keep it up and you won't be doing *anything* this summer."

I puffed air out from my cheeks. "Yeah. Okay. Sorry, Mom. It won't happen again. I promise."

"Consider this a warning," she said. "Break a second house rule this summer and you're immediately grounded. No T pass."

If you only knew how many house rules I've broken this summer, I thought. But I knew better than to speak. I smiled, instead. "Got it, Mom," I finally replied, when it was obvious that she was waiting for me to say something.

"I brought sandwiches home for dinner," she said. "Wash up and come down." She turned and headed down the stairs.

Quickly, I checked my room: album put away, photo in envelope. I tucked the envelope between my mattress and box spring for safekeeping.

Now, how was I going to find millions of dollars of art hidden in the busiest—and probably most well-guarded—building in the state?

16

That night, I barely slept.

First, I waited till a little after midnight, to ensure Mom had conked out, so I could do a quick search of some of the random storage areas in our house. I was pretty sure that Grumps wouldn't have packed up zillions of dollars of art and stuck it in our eaves, but, as Nini says, "Why jump over the fence when your own backyard bears exploring?"

So I grabbed my flashlight and hit the cupboard under the stairs (no wizard boy or stolen art—just our winter jackets, clothes, and Christmas decorations) and the eaves storage in the hallway outside my bedroom (dusty boxes wrapped in green-and-white twine labeled TAX RECEIPTS, ANNE'S ROOM, and MISC—HOUSEHOLD.) Although in theory Grumps could have hidden at least *some* of the Gardner art in one or two of the boxes, it didn't seem likely. Mom and Nini did actually put stuff in there, and I didn't think Grumps would take the chance that they'd accidentally find something they weren't supposed to.

I crept out from the eaves as quietly as possible, closing its Hobbit-door behind me, and clicked the flashlight off. Was there any place I was missing?

Leaning my head against the bathroom door, I closed my eyes and visualized my house: three floors, with Mom and me taking up the second and third levels. Nini's apartment didn't have a lot of extra closet space—there were two bedrooms, a kitchen, bathroom, dining room, and den—and she and Grumps stored most of their extra stuff in the basement. Right away, I realized that the basement would be a bad hiding place. It was damp and musty-smelling, and Nini frequently moved stuff around down there, keeping an eye out for mold.

In our apartment, I'd gone through the two most obvious hiding places. The main level had the kitchen/dining room, a den, Mom's bedroom, and her bathroom. The third floor was my bedroom and bathroom . . . and a tiny attic space. I'd nearly forgotten about it because the door was blocked by a giant, tree-like house plant that Mom'd stuck in the hallway. And I was standing straight across from it.

I put the flashlight down and grabbed the pot. It was heavier than it looked, but slid across the floor pretty easily. When I opened the door and stepped into the attic, I didn't see much of anything—an old bike, a few boxes wrapped in that same green twine (Grumps had a giant ball of it that he used to fasten anything and everything), and one of those hanging bags for suits and dresses.

Out of curiosity, I aimed my flashlight at the bag and unzipped.

After swatting at a big plume of dust, I beamed the flashlight inside:

A yellowed dress, lace-covered at the chest, with short ruffled sleeves and a high neckline. For a second, I couldn't place it—then I realized I was looking at Nini's wedding dress. There was a picture downstairs in her apartment of her and Grumps on their wedding day—him in a black suit, her in the dress, standing on the steps of the church our family still goes to. I wondered if she knew what she was getting into when she married him. It was something I'd never asked Grumps, and Nini didn't like to talk about "that part" of their life— every time she heard Grumps telling me a story, she tightened her lips into a line and shook her head. I just assumed that it made her uncomfortable, but now I wondered how much she *really* knew—about everything.

Did *she*—a chill fluttered down my back in the stifling attic—know where the art was?

I swallowed. I'd watched enough cop shows and Tru-Crime TV to learn about forensic psychology to know that if Nini *was* in on some of that info, it made her just as much a criminal as Grumps.

I zipped up the bag, discouraged and disappointed, ready to head back to bed. As I turned to the door, the flashlight beam revealed something sticking up from one of the floor-boards: a loop of that green-and-white twine.

I almost walked past it. I almost left it alone. I almost pretended I didn't see it.

But I did.

I crouched, stuck one finger through the loop, and tugged.

The floorboard came up without a sound. Underneath it was a big empty space in the floor, wider than the board I'd removed. And tucked inside was a wrapped bundle. My heart stuttered. Had Grumps actually hidden some of the art *in our house?* Although the space was too small for the paintings or the sketches, the vase-thing and the flagpole eagle could be right in front of me.

Carefully, I put the flashlight at the edge of the opening and reached into the hiding place. The bundle was lumpy and wrapped in a soft cloth. I tugged on it gently, and something clinked. The cloth pulled back and it glinted. I aimed the beam on it. Instead of an eagle or a vase, I'd uncovered . . . a teapot.

A *teapot?*

Darkly tarnished, but it was definitely silver. It had a long spout and was engraved with curlicues and flowery designs. I shifted the wrapping and saw two other, smaller silver objects: a bowl and a pitcher. Sugar and cream?

I rocked back on my heels. Clearly, this was not anything related to the Gardner art. But I was pretty sure that Nini wouldn't have had Grumps store a classy family heirloom under the attic floor. Logically, that left only one other option: The tea set was also stolen property.

But from what?

For a minute, I let myself consider figuring it out: Going back to my room, firing up Google, taking a photo of the tea set, searching for its home, and returning it to wherever it belonged.

And then I got tired. Like, really, really tired. How much could I actually do? This week, I had five million dollars in stolen art to track down and a gangster after me. The rest of the summer? Forget the best summer ever—I'd be happy hanging out like a normal kid with Ollie before I had to don the Uniform of Horror. The tea set could wait.

I repacked it, wrapping the cloth tightly, and tucked it back into the floor cubby. Next, I replaced the board and left the piece of twine sticking up . . . just in case I decided to come back for it some other time. While I went through each step, I stayed super-laser-beam-focused on what I was doing. Because if I didn't, really awful questions peppered my brain. Questions like:

How much more was hidden in this house?

Was Grumps honest with *anyone*?

Did Nini know about this stuff? Did my *mom?*!

You know, family things that I'm sure every kid thinks about on hot nights in June.

I closed the attic door behind me and replaced the plant. Then I ducked into the bathroom to splash some water on my face and cool off. The deeper I got into this Gardner stuff, the more I hated what it showed me about the people I thought I knew best.

Back in my bedroom, I collapsed on my bed and pulled out the proof. I went over each line, trying to figure out how in the heck I would get into the state house to look for the art—or where in the state house it might be. No matter what scenario I came up with—from a disguise (seriously. At one point I thought a *disguise* might work—that's desperation, right there) to hiding behind some drapes to just asking where my grandfather had worked—every one led back to the same place: Getting caught and going to juvie. And although I don't *exactly* know what I want to do with my life, I can totally tell you that spending time in prison would *not* be on any list I'd come up with. Ever.

So all I got from those efforts were bleary eyes, a muzzy head, and more frustration. No wonder Sully Cupcakes hadn't been able to find—or get his hands on—the art. Grumps didn't mess around with where he'd put it (*or anything else, for that matter,* I thought, remembering the silver tea set across the hall).

Later that morning, on the way downstairs, I had to admit it. No matter what crazy scheme I'd come up with, there was only one solution: Ask Nini or Grumps what he'd done at the state house and hope they told me the truth.

"You look awful."

I was almost at the bottom step and jumped about eight thousand feet at the words. I stumbled and scrabbled at the banister for balance, but I still landed on my ankle funny.

"Sheesh, Mom!" I snapped, ankle burning. She was sitting at the kitchen table, directly across from the staircase, sections of the newspaper spread around her like fallen flower petals and wearing her Mighty Mighty Bosstones Hometown Throwdown T-shirt from, like, 2001. "What are you doing here? Is everything okay?" I limped down the last step and crossed to the kitchen, making straight for the coffeepot.

"I know you tend to forget I live here too," Mom said, raising an eyebrow as I filled the biggest mug we had with coffee and a metric ton of sugar, "but we have a wake tonight. I don't go to work till two when we have a wake." She said the last part in a slow, careful voice, the way you'd speak to a possibly dangerous animal or a freaked-out toddler.

"Oh," I mumbled. Mom acted as a kind of hostess during the funeral home's wakes—directing relatives where to go, refilling the tissue supply, encouraging people to sign the guest book—which meant staying until the last relatives left. Her bosses always let her come in late those days. Great for her, but this could be a problem for me. I took a swig from the mug, burning my mouth for the second time in two days. On the plus side, the searing pain made me more alert.

"That's hot," Mom pointed out.

"Thanks," I wheezed. "Figured that out." I plopped the cup on the table and slumped into the seat across from her.

"Didn't sleep well?"

I shook my head and yawned so wide, my jaw cracked. The wake was a problem, because Mom would be home all morning, making it hard for me to get out without getting quizzed.

"I thought we could take a ride to shop for your Boston Classics uniform this morning," Mom added, once I stopped yawning. "We may as well, while we have the time."

Uniform of Horror time—this meant we'd be staying in Boston! But I'd lose time searching for the art.

Be careful what you wish for, right?

17

I texted Ollie before leaving, hoping that he could figure out a way into the state house while I was gone. It seemed like the bad luck was contagious, though, as he had to babysit LeeLee for the morning; her summer program was temporarily closed thanks to a leaking air conditioner. His mom took advantage of the day off to run errands.

Search your house last nite? he texted. *Find any treasure? LOL!*

If you only knew. For a second, I considered telling him. But—just like I'd realized the night before—the idea of starting another mystery was exhausting. Maybe I wasn't destined for a career in forensic psychology or law enforcement after all.

Oh yeah. *Tunz*, I wrote back, then tossed my phone onto my bed.

"Margaret Mildred, get the lead out!" my mom hollered from downstairs.

"Coming!" I yelled back. I ignored the use of my real name. *Hoping that'll get to me?* I thought. *You have no idea . . .*

We'd spent nearly an hour in a small, dusty uniform store in South Boston, where I got to try on the navy blue polo shirt, plaid skirt, and super-stylish khaki pants that I'd be wearing to Boston Classics this fall. Although I took our shopping trip as a great sign that we'd be staying in Massachusetts, the lowlight came when Jolie Pearson and her mom also showed up—and I realized she'd be attending high school with me.

Now, over lunch, Mom was trying to grill me about Jolie— "just a girl from school . . . she thinks she's all that . . . no, Mom, she doesn't bully me"—but there wasn't much to say. If you want the truth, it's me who annoys her more, I'd bet. But I didn't tell Mom that.

"Well, if you change your mind about going there this fall, let me know. We have other options."

"What does that mean?"

Mom shrugged. "Just . . . you know. Other options. If you'd rather go somewhere else."

I shook my head, stomach tight. I didn't like how this was going.

"Hey . . ." I said, trying for a subject change. "So I've been looking at the photo album that Nini and Grumps gave me. It's pretty cool."

Mom nodded. "I bet."

"He worked at so many places downtown, I can't believe it."

She just nodded again. It's always like this—every time I bring up Grumps, Mom gets all awkward and uncomfortable, like I'm talking about someone else's father, not her own. She nibbled a French fry.

"Do you remember him doing a job at the state house?"

She didn't say anything for a second, just made that fry last. Her dark hair was pulled back into a low ponytail, and for a second I saw her not as my mom, but as someone else might see her, and how young she was—after all, she had me when she was eighteen. And she seemed really, really sad. She finally swallowed the fry.

"I was in elementary school," she said. She creased her napkin, not looking at me. "He took me and Nini on a 'behind the scenes' tour of the building at one point while he was there. We met the governor, saw a bunch of offices, and went to a storeroom under the dome where he was replacing the floor and some beams. Not the most exciting thing for a fourth grader, but my teacher loved hearing about it. I got a gold star on Monday." She popped another fry in her mouth.

Not the most exciting thing for you, I thought, but for me . . . well, this was Jackpot City. I stayed cool, though.

"Oh. Neat." I was about to ask her another question, but Mom beat me to it.

"Ready? I have to get home so I can get ready for work." We had plenty of time, but it was obvious that this conversation was over. I scarfed the last few fries on my plate, and we headed out.

And now I totally had a plan.

18

When we got home, I zoomed upstairs to text Ollie. I'd left my phone on my bed, and it was nearly out of battery. So I had to spend fifteen minutes frantically searching for the charger before I could finally send him the message.

Think I have r site. Can you get out tonite?

And then there was the excruciating wait until he texted me back.

Yes. Rents owe me. I Scooby Doo'ed all morning. Where?

I sent him the details and asked him to figure out a way in. Although I'm sure the family of the deceased was heartbroken, I was now grateful that Mom had to work that wake. I'd be in the clear until ten, if I checked in with Nini before I left. The Sox were playing Cleveland tonight, and she'd be parked in front of the game, not caring what I was doing.

Then it was just a matter of killing time. I pulled out the proof and added a line to the statements column: *Possible hiding place: state house storeroom.* Under reasons, I wrote: *Brought Mom and Nini there on tour.*

Of course, I could be wrong. I mean, if Grumps had access to the whole state house, what were the odds that he would bring them specifically to the place where he hid the Gardner art? On the other hand . . . if they'd gone on the tour before March 18, there was no reason why he *wouldn't* have shown them the storeroom.

I hopped online to check the state house hours: We had until 3:30 to get on a tour, or we could just go in on our own. The building closed at 4:30.

Oh.

That didn't give us much time to find the art and get something out.

It was like Ollie read my mind. My phone buzzed.

"There's no way we can get the stuff out by four," he said, without even saying hello.

"I know."

"Today we'll do recon," he said. "We'll go in, take the tour, check it out, make a plan, and go back tomorrow."

Time was slipping away, but I knew he was right. The only thing worse than not finding the art in time to hand it over to Sully Cupcakes and The Redhead was getting caught breaking and entering into one of the most famous buildings in the country.

We hung up, and I grabbed my bike bag and packed it with necessities: a notebook and pencil, my camera, the proof, cash, phone, and an apple. Mom caught me in the kitchen— she was dressed in a dark suit, hair in a twist, makeup on; looking grown-up and completely different than she had at lunch. I told her I was heading into town with Ollie—to Park Street and the Public Garden, which was not really a lie.

"We're going to look for a cache," I explained.

She reminded me to abide by the rules, and took off.

Ollie and I left shortly thereafter, bumping into town on the Orange Line. He'd made reservations for us on the last state house tour of the day. We jogged up the stairs—the same ones Grumps had stood on in the photo—and met the tour group at the door.

For forty-five minutes, we snapped pictures, touched woodwork, and admired the oil paintings of past Massachusetts governors and studied the statues that dotted the halls. There were a couple of other kids with their parents in the group, and they kept giving us funny looks like they couldn't believe how into it we were.

If you only knew why, I thought.

By the time the tour was over, I had a pretty good idea of the layout of the building, but no clue where that storeroom would be. Ollie and I left the group and crossed into the Common, where we grabbed lemonades at the Frog Pond stand and found a patch of grass under a tree.

"To treasure hunting," I said, holding up my plastic cup.

"To treasure *finding*," he responded. We clicked cups and sipped.

"So?" Ollie asked, after we'd sat in silence for a minute.

I gulped some more icy lemonade. "So I have no idea what we're going to do. I couldn't even find the storeroom. The tour guide never mentioned it."

He grinned. "Really? It's a hidden door, but not hidden *that* well." He described a section of the third-floor hallway that we'd gone through. Again, I was amazed by what Ollie *saw*. It was like he was in a different world than the rest of us. How could he pick out a camouflaged door after walking past it once?

"Cool . . . so, we think we have the door . . . now what?"

"We hide," he said slowly, thinking it through. "There's no other way to do it. We're going to have to get in before they close, like today, and hide somewhere. Then, when it's dark, we can go up to the storeroom."

I didn't like the idea—too much could go wrong—but I didn't respond right away. Were there other options?

Probably not.

"What about security cameras and stuff?" I asked, finally.

"I'll look into that," Ollie said. "The cache boards are filled with people who are experts at getting around security to hide stuff. Someone will have a tip."

"Don't let any of your online buddies know what we're up to," I said. I hated to say it out loud—it was like I didn't trust him or something—but I was sure of this: Those "urban treasure hunters" would be all over the Gardner art search. There was probably a group of them working on it right now!

"Cross my heart," he said solemnly.

I laughed, but hearing him say that really did make me feel better.

We spent the rest of the afternoon as though there were no such things as The Redhead, or the Gardner museum, or a ticking clock: ate ice cream on Newbury Street, did some window-shopping, and bummed around downtown. Ollie *did* find a cache in Copley Square park—and climbed on the back of the tortoise statue to proclaim his "mad skillz" after he found it—so my lie to my mom ended up not being a lie after all.

It was a taste of the summer I *thought* we'd have—the summer I *wanted* to have after all of this was finished.

But the longer this went on, the more I realized that my summer would never be what I thought it would.

19

My luck held out the next day. Mom went in to work a little late, and called just after noon with the news that they'd be receiving a body late in the afternoon. She'd need to meet with the family that evening. Although she wouldn't be out as late as she would if there was a wake, I quickly told her that Ollie and I had plans to see a movie, and could I come home around 10:30? She was fine with it.

The day dragged. I repacked my bike bag a bunch of times, adding a flashlight and a bottle of water to the stuff that had been in there the day before.

Finally, Ollie and I met and hopped on the T. We didn't say much. I didn't know about him, but I was a mix of nervous, excited, terrified, and wishing we hadn't done this.

"I got some info for us," he said as the train clacked into Back Bay Station.

"Cool," I said. A bunch of people got on and stood near us, though, so Ollie didn't say anything until we reached our stop: Downtown Crossing. We walked through the tunnel connecting it to Park Street Station, and came out on the street just a block away from the state house.

"All we have to do is get into a conference room," he said. "Although they have cameras and security in the halls, they can't record what goes on in the committee discussions unless it's via a state-appointed recorder. So we hide out in a conference room until dark. And since we're going in at the end of the day . . ."

"There shouldn't be any meetings happening!" I finished for him.

"Exactly."

We were standing at the foot of the steps by this point. Today's tour group was larger. It allowed us to blend in a little more.

When the group reached the third floor, where a lot of the meeting rooms were, Ollie and I drifted toward the back of the crowd. When we passed a particularly beautiful oil painting next to a conference room, we paused to admire it. The group kept going.

I twisted the doorknob. It spun, no problem. The tour turned a corner.

"Go!" I whispered.

Ollie and I ducked in, and I pulled the door closed quietly behind us. The room had no windows; a big table stretched away from the door, and huge black chairs crowded around it. We each curled up in one, Ollie across the table from me. We swiveled the backs of the chairs to the door, and with our feet off the ground, no one could see us.

"Bet you didn't have this in mind when you were planning the best summer ever," Ollie whispered.

"You mean the gangsters, art thefts, and breaking into state property?" I tucked my feet under me more tightly. "Oh yeah, totally on my list.

"I've given up on the best summer ever," I added. "I just want us to survive July without getting killed or arrested."

Ollie laughed. "Admit it. Even though it's scary, it is also pretty awesome—the ultimate treasure hunt." Even separated by the sea of table, I could see the excitement on Ollie's face.

He was right. It *was* pretty awesome.

"Agreed."

We were quiet for a minute, and Ollie swiveled his chair back and forth.

"Can I ask you something, Mox?"

"Sure."

He scratched under his glasses. "Do you think I'm making the right choice—about Chestnut Prep?"

That was *not* what I expected to hear. Ever since I met Ollie, he said that's where he was going to high school. It was one of the best schools in the state, and had *the* best science program. MIT, Ollie's dream college, offered a full scholarship to one senior from CCP every year. Ollie would totally win.

"Um, I didn't even think it *was* a choice," I said. "I thought you were programmed from birth to go there. You're going to do awesome."

He flushed. "Thanks. I just . . . it's weird, you know? I mean, I'll know a few people from the troop, but still . . ."

"You'll be fine," I said. It's funny, but hearing Ollie say that he was nervous made me feel so much better about Boston Classics.

"Besides," he added. "Not that it'll matter. We'll both be taking correspondence classes from jail."

"Now *that* is truly the Uniform of Horror," I said. "Orange is so *not* disco."

We grinned at each other, then settled in to wait.

And wait. And wait.

One thing I never considered about sneaking into buildings? If you're hiding, you really can't go to the bathroom. And two hours into our wait, I had to pee. Ollie—smart kid—had fallen asleep, but I was too uncomfortable.

I checked the time on my phone: 6:34. Should I chance sneaking out and running to the ladies' room down the hall? What about the surveillance cameras? I pulled on my lower lip.

If I got caught and Ollie was still in dreamland, he'd have no idea what was going on when he woke.

By seven, I was considering emptying my water bottle and, well . . . refilling it. Luckily, Ollie woke up before I got that drastic.

"We should be in the clear," he said, "except for the cleaning crew. We can run into the hall and you can do your thing before we go upstairs. Stick close to the walls so you'll have less chance of being seen by the cameras."

I was grateful to have the opportunity, but nervous too.

We waited a few more minutes—until just after seven. Ollie opened the door and we peeked into the hallway.

Totally clear.

I scooted down to the ladies', and when I was finished, I peeked out the door and spotted Ollie, crouched underneath a big old desk against the opposite wall. He brought his finger to his lips and pointed up to a camera panning the hall. When it was pointed the other way, I raced over to him and slid in on my knees, straight out of an action movie. Apparently unimpressed by my entrance, Ollie watched the camera.

"Let's go," he whispered.

A few steps down the hall, and we were at the camouflaged storeroom door. Ollie twisted a funny knob, and we found ourselves at the bottom of a stairwell, no cameras in sight.

We crept up the dusty stairs, flashlights brightening the gloom. With each step, the temperature in the narrow space increased by about five degrees. I wiped the sweat off my forehead. It was hard to breathe. Behind me, Ollie smothered his 576th sneeze.

"You are *so* going to get us caught," I whispered.

He honked into a tissue. "'Cause that's part of my plan," he mumbled, sounding filled to the gills with snot. "At least I don't have to pee!"

He had me there.

Even though he couldn't see me, I smiled. A few more steps—and muffled sneezes—later, we came to one of those heavy fire doors. Ollie squeezed next to me. We shined our lights on the big sign screwed into the metal door: AUTHO-RIZED PERSONNEL ONLY.

"Do you think there's an alarm too?"

"Not according to my sources," he replied. Ollie swung his flashlight around the perimeter of the frame. "Can't tell, anyway," he responded after a second. "Hinges are on the other side." A crash bar, just like the one on the caf door at school, bisected the door below the sign. Ollie mopped his face with a red bandanna.

"On three?" I asked, half hoping he'd talk me out of it, half hoping this was just a dream . . . all the way hoping that we would know what to do if the art was on the other side. Ollie grunted. We put our hands on the bar.

"One . . . two . . ." I took a deep breath. "Three!" We pushed.

It opened without even a squeak.

Ollie and I had put so much of our weight into it, we nearly fell into the room. Our flashlights stabbed the dark in all directions, like a laser-light planetarium show. I grabbed the doorframe and steadied myself. Ollie directed his flashlight to the wall.

"What are you looking for?"

"Light switch," he said. "There're no windows up here. It's safe." As soon as he said that, his light found one of those multi-switch control panels. Six switches, all turned to the off position. He reached out and flipped the first one. Nothing happened.

The second—same thing. My hands were turning into sweat waterfalls.

Switch number three: jackpot.

I blinked at the brightness.

We were standing on the edge of a massive storeroom at the top of the state house. Boxes and crates were stacked against the walls, objects covered with sheets and tarps dotted the floor, and the wall to our right was jammed with rows and rows of metal filing cabinets.

I inhaled the hot, stale air and stepped in, tugging Ollie with me. He turned around and wedged his flashlight in the doorjamb.

"In case it locks behind us or something," he said.

"Nice," I responded. I hadn't thought of that. And with the door (mostly) closed, I didn't feel the need to whisper anymore. "Where do we start?"

Ollie walked into the middle of the room, head turning in every direction. "Where would you put priceless art?" he asked.

I considered all we thought we knew about the theft, Grumps, and Sully Cupcakes. "There's a lot of stuff, so I'd probably box it and put it where people wouldn't look very often."

Ollie nodded, and walked over to some boxes and crates. "These are the state house Christmas decorations," he said.

"Those come out every year."

"Thank you, Captain Obvious," Ollie responded. He sneezed again. Although his words ruffled my feathers, they also made me feel better.

I glanced around the room and headed straight across

from the door. As I walked, I peered at the boxes. Some were dated and labeled, some were blank, some were those boxes that copy machine paper come in, and by the looks of the writing on them, were pretty old. Ollie, probably anticipating what I was going to do, squeezed in between a few boxes near the Christmas decorations and started rummaging.

The stuff at the far side of the room was definitely old—a few boxes were dated 1964, others were from the '70s and '80s. All were covered in a thick, gritty gray dust. I sneezed.

"Bless you," Ollie called from across the room, in a voice sweeter than syrup and designed to show me how . . . *magnanimous* he was. I scowled in his general direction and went back to work.

What was I looking for? Grumps wouldn't have labeled the paintings GARDNER MUSEUM—MARCH 1990 or anything. He was up here to replace some floorboards and structural beams, but the art was way too big to put in a hidey-hole in the floor . . .

Then I saw it. Wedged between a big wooden crate and a cardboard box, there was an old-looking dusty dresser. The drawers were tied shut with the same green-and-white twine that Grumps kept in his toolbox—and that I'd found in my own attic. I squirmed through the cardboard maze, trying to get closer. Ollie sneezed again.

All that was between me and the dresser was a giant carton of "Time Sheets—1988." I stretched my arm out, fingers grazing the drawer handles, and tried to open one. It gave a little, then stopped. The twine was tied tight.

"I think I found it!" I called to Ollie, my voice hoarse. I didn't turn around, but I heard him slide against boxes and crates, crossing the room.

"How do you know?"

I pointed to the green twine. "That's all over stuff at our house."

"Can we get it out?"

I wiped my moist palms on my now-grimy skirt. "I think we need to cut it." I grabbed a handle and tugged, leaning awkwardly over the box at my feet. Again, that same resistance. The handles were tied together, so the drawers couldn't open.

"Here," Ollie muttered. He bent and lifted the box of time sheets out of the way, straining with the effort. We squeezed in front of the dresser.

"This seems like a risky spot, don't you think?" he asked. "Someone could have moved this or taken it to the Dumpster."

I nodded. "Yeah. But Grumps must have known that it would stay put, otherwise he wouldn't have chosen it."

Ollie dug out his house key and sawed through the twine. It came apart pretty easily, and we unthreaded the rope from the handles. We stepped back. I didn't know about him, but my heart was slamming harder than Joey Kramer's bass drum at the end of "Living on the Edge."

"Ready to open it?" I asked. Back to whispering. What is it about searching for stolen art that makes me whisper?

Ollie chewed his lower lip. "I guess so. What should we do with it if we find something? Leave it? Take it? And how would we get it out of here?"

I hadn't figured that part out yet. I stared at the dresser. Dark wood, carved with a little pinecone on the top of it. Nothing special.

"Let's do it."

"All right," Ollie said. I hadn't realized I'd said it out loud, but there you go.

"One drawer at a time," I said. No whisper that time.

Ollie caught on. "Yeah."

I grasped the first of the six drawer handles. It squeaked and opened.

And it was empty. So were the next two. And then . . . in drawer number four—a brown-paper-wrapped package, tied with the green-and-white twine.

"Got it!" Triumphant, I held it up. It was a little more than a foot square, and heavier than it looked. The twine was wrapped around it like you'd see on a birthday present—dividing the top of the paper into four squares, the bow in the middle.

"Best. Birthday. Present. Ever."

"Totally," Ollie agreed.

I handed him the package. Carefully, Ollie holding it with two hands, I cut the twine with my house key and stuck a fingernail into the paper, right at the corner, and slid it down the seam, opening a pocket. Then I went back to the top, and did the same thing to two other sides, slicing the edge of the wrapping so we could fold it back, but not enough so it would flap open on its own.

We were about to see something the world was waiting for.

20

We saw plywood. Plain, boring plywood. My heart plummeted down the three floors we'd just climbed. If the stuff wasn't here, then where? All of a sudden I realized how little time I had left.

"Look," Ollie said. "There're two of them." He pointed to the corner, where—sure enough—there were two pieces of plywood wrapped together.

"D'oh!" I slapped my hand to my forehead, feeling like a total idiot. "Of course!" The art needed to be protected, and you couldn't just roll it up—it was too fragile. Making a priceless art sandwich was probably the best thing Grumps could think of to do.

He'd also wrapped them so tightly together that it was nearly impossible to pry them apart without splitting open the whole package. But we needed proof.

Ollie held the paper while I slid the piece of plywood out, leaving the bottom piece and the artwork behind. Finally—finally!—we were rewarded. One of the pieces, a watercolor of a crowd, was on top. Sketches—there were five of them—were in the bundle. Ollie pulled a folded sheet of paper from his pocket: the flyer with the images of the stolen art off the Gardner website.

We were looking at a Degas. *La Sortie de Pesage*, to be exact. Watercolor and pencil.

"We found it! Oh my god, we found it," I gasped, totally geeking out. Unexpected relief rushed through me. It was over. My knees sagged a little bit. Ollie grabbed my arm, eyes frowning behind his glasses.

"Don't keel over yet," he said. "This isn't all of it. Not even close."

After I'd gotten over thinking that it was totally over—and it totally wasn't—Ollie and I sat on the dusty floor and leaned against one of the crates.

"There just isn't enough room in that dresser," he pointed out. "All six of the small works are in there, but thirteen items were stolen—some are really big paintings."

He was right, of course. And inside, I totally knew everything he was saying before he said it. But hearing it out loud was something else entirely.

"Should we look around some more?" I asked.

Ollie cocked his head at me.

"Yeah, yeah . . ." I muttered. I glanced at the time displayed on my cell phone. It was late, and we still had to get out of here and get home before our parents got suspicious. But I couldn't just walk away from the small works and leave them. Plus—oh yeah, minor details—*we were sitting in the attic of the state house* after hours and had to sneak out. Yeah.

I pulled the proof from my pocket, and added *Etchings and watercolor found in state house* to the reasons column.

"What should we do with them?"

I shrugged. I hadn't thought that far ahead. I mean, we'd found *some* of them—but now what? Wait around for The Redhead? Call the police? I wrestled with the options. Part of me never expected to actually find anything, I guess.

"We have to hide them somewhere," I said finally. "There's no way we can leave them here, and I'm not sure what to do with them yet."

Out of the corner of my eye, I saw Ollie nod. It was our best choice—I knew that—but it still freaked me out. We'd be hiding the art again, which was some kind of criminal act, I was sure of that.

Ollie and I stood and dusted off.

"Hey, Moxie?" Ollie said. I stopped swiping at my skirt and turned to him. He was wearing a huge, face-splitting grin. "Can we just take a moment here?"

"Uh, sure?"

Ollie raised his hand for a high five. "*We found some of the Gardner art! We found millions of dollars of stolen property!*" I slapped his hand, and we fist-bumped too. I couldn't stop smiling now either.

"We are pretty disco right now," he added.

I laughed. "We are *so* disco, we make disco cooler than it ever was."

We continued our little celebration for another minute, then it was back to the business of re-hiding the formerly stolen art.

"Maybe we should put them somewhere else in the room," I suggested.

"Negatory," Ollie replied. "First rule of hiding something: Put it where no one can find it. We found this, and it's pretty obvious that we've been in here." He gestured to the smeary dust and tracks all over the floor. "Anyone who comes up here would find this stuff in a second."

Although I bet that no one came to the storeroom once the holiday decorations were put away, I could see Ollie's point . . . and didn't want to risk losing what we found if The Redhead decided to check this place out.

"So let's find a better hiding spot," I said. "That's your department."

Eyes wide behind his glasses, Ollie nodded. The package easily fit in his messenger bag. To keep it safe, he wedged it between a book and leftover history folder. Not how priceless art is usually moved, I bet.

While Ollie shuffled the contents of his bag, I kept an eye on the clock. It was late and my anxiety level climbed as high as the Prudential tower.

"Hey." He gestured to the box of time sheets he'd moved. "Let's put this back." We each grabbed a side, and on three, heaved.

Moving paperwork is harder—and heavier—than you'd think. It took us a minute to get the box to its old home, and the stifling air didn't help our speed. Ollie also insisted that we drag our feet over the floor, to cover our tracks. I pointed out that our literal tracks—footprints—were visible in the dust.

"We've walked all over this room," he said. He sneezed, then wiped his nose (for the snot) and forehead (for the sweat). "No one will be able to tell where we went to do what, but we don't want this area to look suspicious. Let's cover the dresser with this." We tugged a sheet covering a nearby table over the dresser. It didn't hide the whole thing, but helped set the scene of "ancient stuff that's never been touched."

So, to review: Priceless artwork—check. Coming out of attic—check. Escape plan? Not so much.

It was nearly nine thirty, and I had to be home in one hour.

"How are we going to get out of here?" Ollie asked. He handed me the bag holding the art.

"No pressure—just carrying around millions of dollars of stolen property," I joked. Lamely. "I do it every day."

"How are we going to get out of here?" he repeated.

"Carefully," I answered. On our way in, it was easy—we could claim to be lost kids, searching for our parents/camp tour group/whatever, and security would probably have brought us to the front of the building without thinking about it. But now? Hours after closing to the public, when—I glanced at my dirt-smeared skirt and hands, and Ollie's dusty T-shirt and shorts—we were filthy and covered in suspicion, if security found us we'd be headed straight for a lot of questions.

"I figured as much. We should've planned this part better," he added.

There wasn't much we could do about that now. Ollie

retrieved his flashlight at the door. I clicked the overhead light off and we switched the flashlights back on.

"Quiet," Ollie whispered. He eased the storeroom door open wide enough for us to slip through and we crossed onto the staircase. The door closed behind us with a click.

Eyes growing used to the gloom again, we moved in complete silence. It should've been easier now that we knew where we were going, but it wasn't. I held my breath with every step, afraid we'd be caught. We crept down those stairs slower than Big Papi rounding the bases at Fenway.

Finally, we reached the bottom door. As nerve-racking as this flight of stairs was, that was the easy part. Once we opened this door, we'd be back in the main part of the state house—and avoiding people and cameras.

"Ready?" Ollie's whisper was so low, at first I thought he was just breathing heavy. He stifled a sneeze.

I nodded. We shut off the flashlights; I reached out with a hand that may or may not have been shaking, and grasped the knob, gently twisting it while pushing my shoulder into the door. It opened smoothly. I stepped out.

I should've thought to check the hall first.

21

The gray-suited man had passed the door and entered a room at the far end of the hall. It didn't matter. Needles peppered my whole body with fear. I gasped and jumped back into the stairwell, crashing into Ollie, bag bumping around my middle. Luckily, Ollie didn't fall over—just let out a big "oof!" I grabbed his shoulder to keep myself standing. I could feel his heart hammering too.

"What is the matter with you?" he whisper-snapped. The stairwell was pitch-black without our flashlights on.

"There was a *guy* out there." I took my hand back. I was pretty sure it was shaking. I was pretty sure that I had never been this terrified in my life. *Deep breaths*, Moxie, I told myself. *Calm down.*

"We have to peek first." Ollie squeezed around me and opened the door a crack. "I think he's gone. Quick!"

He darted out onto the hallway's cushy rug. I was still trying to calm my crazy nerves. He tugged me out anyway.

The door closed, and we were standing, exposed, in the plush hall. *That* brought me to my senses. We raced to the far end, back to the main staircase, keeping close to the wall, and hid in an alcove. There was no conversation at this point—it was just get out and get out *fast*. Hopefully we'd be just a blur on the security cameras. It was too late to worry about that now.

The stairs were clear. We rattled down them, into the main foyer of the building. The statues' and paintings' eyes bored into me.

Without stopping, we ran across the tile floor, sneakers squeaking, the bag around my body flapping. I'm faster than Ollie, and I reached the front door first, arms outstretched. Then, I heard it:

"Hey! Kids! Wait!"

I didn't even turn my head, just burst through the door and into the night air. Ollie puffed. I launched off the top step, feet only touching the ground twice more down the stairs, and didn't stop until I crossed Beacon Street and landed in the Common. Ollie pounded the pavement behind me. I turned around once I hit grass.

Red-faced and still puffing, Ollie was moving as fast as his asthma would let him. I couldn't see anyone else coming down the state house steps, so I figured we were in the clear.

Ollie passed me and didn't stop until he was closer to Park Street Station, where he collapsed on a bench and fished around in his pockets for his inhaler. He took a couple of sucks off it while I checked the contents of the bag. Everything was fine.

"You okay?"

He nodded, head hanging down between his knees, sweat dripping onto the sidewalk.

I sat, waiting, replaying the whole incident in my mind: creeping into the building, finding the right door and the storeroom, then our escape. Running across the floor and my leap off the top of the state house steps? Not classy. Or smooth. Or disco.

I couldn't help it, the image struck me as funny. A giggle escaped, and once I started, I just couldn't stop. Ollie, breathing better, turned to me. His black spiky hair was tinged gray at the tips from dust, and there was a cobweb stuck to his shoulder. "*You* okay?"

I was laughing so hard, I could only nod.

"It's not funny!" he cried. "We could've gotten caught . . ." His voice trickled off, and the corners of his mouth twitched . . . which only made me laugh harder.

He started too. Soon, we were both wiping away tears from laughing so hard.

"Reaction to stress," Ollie gasped, which sent me howling again.

"Stupid kids," some college punk muttered to his friend as they walked by.

"Use your self-defense moves on 'em, Mox," Ollie said between bouts of laughing. "Protect me!" Grumps taught me self-defense starting in second grade. He said since I went to school in the city, I needed to know how to take care of myself.

For some reason, this made us laugh even harder. My stomach hurt.

Finally, our hilarity slowed into hiccups and the occasional giggle.

"Oh my god," I said, wiping my eyes, "oh my god."

"I know," said Ollie. He took a hit off his inhaler and checked the time. "Oh my god! We have to get home!"

I had twenty minutes to make my curfew, which would take a miracle of public transportation. We booked it into the station and raced through the Orange Line tunnel—more sweating, more puffing, no more laughing.

Something was on our side tonight, though, because a train was waiting when we got there. We didn't say anything as it shot through the dark, but I was pretty sure Ollie was thinking the same thing I was: What were we going to do about the pieces? Had The Redhead been watching us? Did she know we were in the state house? What would she do if she knew we had the art?

Even though I was supposed to be finding the art for Sully and The Redhead, handing it over seemed so wrong. I couldn't figure out what else to do, though—if I gave them what they wanted, they weren't going to return it. And now that I had it—some of the pieces, anyway—I wanted to protect them, crazy as that sounded. Maybe that's why Grumps hid them from Sully Cupcakes in the first place?

The train arrived at our stop, and Ollie and I got off. I had four minutes to get home.

And, I realized, there would be lots of questions about how my clothes got so dirty at the movies.

As we came down the stairs leading to the parking area

and bus stop, I took a deep breath and handed Ollie his messenger bag. He was going to hide the sketches, so he should carry them the rest of the way home. With two stairs to go, I pitched forward, scrabbled for the banister, and missed. I slid onto the asphalt, pain scorching my knees and hands.

"What?! Moxie? You okay?" Ollie helped me up and I blinked tears from my eyes. The heels of my hands were shredded and pocked with pebbles, and my knees trickled blood. A couple of other people stopped to ask if I was okay, and I brushed them off.

"I'm good." I limped to a low wall next to the station and winced when I saw the damage—nothing serious, just ugly. Exactly what I wanted.

"I couldn't go home looking all grimy after a movie, Ollie," I muttered through gritted teeth. "Had to have a reason."

"Jeez, Mox," Ollie said. He handed me a (hopefully clean) tissue and I blotted my bloody knees. "I get you, but that was . . . dramatic. I don't think I can do that."

"You can tell your parents you climbed some dirty wall to get a cache," I pointed out. I balled up the tissue and stuck it in my pocket. My knees and hands were still hot prickles of pain, but I'd be convincing.

"Let's go home."

22

I was right. Mom took one look at my injuries and didn't ask any questions about the movie we were supposed to see or why I was so filthy. I did have to suffer some punishment, though—she sprayed my hands and knees with that stingy antiseptic spray for what felt like thirty minutes.

Freshly bandaged and back in my room, I put on the Mighty Mighty Bosstones and pulled out my proof and Grumps's album. Of course Ollie was right—the paintings wouldn't have fit in that dresser. But were the rest of them in that room, and we missed them? We hadn't checked the place thoroughly—he could've stuck the bigger pieces in some box or something—and we'd never find them. Besides, we'd never be able to go in there again. We'd gotten lucky, getting in and out the way we had.

It couldn't hurt to look at the album some more. There was nothing else I could do from my house anyway. I texted Ollie. His parents had totally bought his caching story.

Chking in2 other options, I sent. *Back 2 album.*

Good idea, he wrote back. *Chking somethng on my end 2. g2g.*

What could that mean?

23

I had every intention of going through the album that night . . . I really did. I climbed onto my bed with it to stretch out and page through its secrets, but the second my body hit the mattress, I had no chance. Exhaustion crept over me like a cozy blanket, and I was out.

I woke up with my face pressed against the cover of the album, the corner leaving a big dent in my cheek. Sunlight filled the room—how late was it? I propped myself up to get a better look at the clock, and winced. My hands and knees still stung, and it felt as though my whole body had been attacked in the night by an army of tiny men with very hard hammers. I ached from head to toe. Could my on-purpose fall have done this? Or was it just the intensity of our escapade? I'd heard stress could do crazy things to the human body. This might be proof.

It was nearly eleven. My mother never lets me sleep that late if she's home. I climbed out of bed and limped downstairs, pausing to brush my teeth and pull my hair back in a ratty ponytail.

Mom had left a note on the table: *Had to go in to work.*

Nini downstairs till Mass. Put new Band-Aids on. MANDA-TORY dinner with Richard, 6 p.m.

Ugh! *Why* wouldn't this dinner thing go away? Along with trying to figure out next steps with the Gardner stuff, I needed to deal with Putrid Richard and the potentially life-altering news he'd spring on me tonight.

Nini typically went to eleven o'clock Mass at the nursing home with Grumps. She'd already left, but if I timed it right, I could look at the album and then maybe meet her there. I had nothing to lose by telling Grumps I'd found the sketches.

I scarfed some breakfast and booked it upstairs as fast as my injured body would allow. The achiness was fading. A hot shower would take care of the rest of it.

My new plan: Talk to Grumps first, go through album second. While I got dressed, I blared the Dropkick Murphys to lighten my mood. So what if I only had a week left to find the rest of the art? No sweat. Ollie and I had found *six pieces* already! Being a detective was a breeze!

I tossed some stuff in a backpack and banged down the stairs and out of the house. Standing on the porch, I propped the screen door open with my elbow and turned to lock the house door. The weight on my arm disappeared as the screen door opened wider. A chill ran up my back. I didn't have to turn around to know who was there.

"Shouldn't you be at church, little girl?" The Redhead purred . . . purred in a "lion about to eat a zebra" sort of way.

I purposely slowed down, taking time to lock the door, hitching my backpack on my shoulder, and then turning to face her.

"Shouldn't you?" I retorted. "Or do you burst into flames when you get inside?"

She made a snarly face at me—a seriously snarly one—and then it was like she caught herself. A cold smile crept across her face.

"Heard that you blasted out of the state house last night," she said. "Interesting place for you and your tubby friend to spend a summer evening. Find anything . . . valuable?"

"We're into American history," I responded. "Field trip." The Redhead's surprise visits were getting old. She was more annoying than scary.

She laughed. "Is that what you call it? Well, just so you know, we'll have that place checked out by tomorrow. If Sully's items are there, tell me now. It'll save us some time. And then I'll go away." She said the last bit playfully, like she was teasing a kitten.

And with a cold, cold knowledge, I realized: No matter what happened with the art, no matter what I did or when I gave them over, The Redhead would never go away—not really. Not to sound straight out of a gangster movie, but I knew too much. Too much about what they'd done, where the art was, and who was involved.

And that was a bad, bad thing.

At least I understood the score. Enough of this. "You can go away *now*," I retorted, and slipped around her to unlock my bike.

"If they're not there, I'll pay your mom or grandmother a visit."

In my head I repeated, *Don't let her get to you. Just don't.*

"Going to see your grandfather?" she asked. "Saying good-bye?"

My back stiffened, but I didn't take her bait. Instead, without turning around to face her, I wheeled my bike off the porch and climbed on. She could stand there all day, for all I cared.

The whole way down our street, I could feel her eyes boring into me. But I never once glanced back.

24

By the time I got to Alton Rivers, I was angry and determined. Realizing that The Redhead would never leave me alone gave me a sense of clarity that I hadn't had before. Part of me knew that all along, I guess, but it was the look in her eye while she was standing on my porch that drove it all home. So I had no choice but to win this game—even though I wasn't sure how.

Angel waved at me as I entered the big common room. He was helping Mrs. Ricci adjust the blue blanket across her lap. Grumps and Nini typically eat brunch together on the porch after church, and that's the direction that Angel tilted his head.

"Thanks!" I called out.

When I stepped outside, Nini and Grumps were sitting at a little table, backs to me. They held hands over the breakfast dishes; she rubbed the back of his hand with her thumb. Together, they looked like any other old couple: cute and cozy, with years of shared history between them. But now I knew better: Grumps had secrets. Lots of them. How could Nini trust him? How much did she know about him, really? The questions made my heart ache.

The door closed behind me with a heavy clump, breaking

their moment and my train of thought, and causing them to look in my direction.

"Moxie!" called Nini. "What a lovely surprise."

A glance at Grumps's face told me everything Nini didn't have to: It was a bad day. His red cheeks drooped a little, and his normally sparkly blue eyes were dull and unfocused. He furrowed his brow.

I crossed the deck and kissed Nini on the top of her head, then squeezed her free hand. Bending my knees, I crouched next to Grumps's wheelchair.

"Hey, Grumps," I said softly. He turned to Nini, confused. "Why she callin' me that?" he asked.

He probably thought I was my mom. "Sorry, Dad," I said, pushing the words past the bowling ball in my chest. These days sucked.

"I'm going to clear the table, Joe," Nini said. When he was like this, it was better to tell him what you were going to do before you did it, so he wouldn't get nervous or more confused. He nodded. Nini stood and stacked their plates. Grumps hadn't finished his eggs—another sign it was a bad day. He loved eggs. I passed her the silverware and crumpled napkins, then held the door open so she could bring their stuff to the kitchen. Even though the staff would totally swoop in and clean, Nini liked to keep busy. Especially on bad days.

This was my chance. Nini would talk to the staff and say hello to other residents on her way back. Although I didn't want to upset him, each minute that passed was like a weight on my back. And Sully and The Redhead probably had worse in mind for him than just a few questions. Not that forcing him to talk would get them answers, I thought. Grumps's body was a shell for whatever his mind believed was real.

I kneeled next to his wheelchair. "I found the Gardner Museum sketches in the state house." Saying it out loud—hearing myself say it—gave me goose bumps. I mean, seriously, *I found millions in stolen art!* How crazy was that?!

Grumps's eyes, which had been in drift mode, sharpened with anger. "You found what—you little . . ." And he rattled off a string of words that white-haired, twinkly-eyed grandfathers are not supposed to know, let alone use on grandchildren.

It's the disease, I told myself. *Just the disease.* Normally, I'd try to calm him down, but I had to get more information. I took a deep breath.

"Are the paintings up there, or did you put them somewhere else?"

Grumps gripped the arm of his chair. His fingers turned white. He raised a shaky hand and pointed it right in my face, leaning so far forward, I thought he was going to topple out of the wheelchair.

"Stay outta there," he growled. "It's not your business. You leave 'em be. Once the limitations run out, we'll talk."

Limitations? That was a word I hadn't heard before. I snuck a glance at the door, hoping Nini would continue chatting and give me some more time.

"Are the paintings in another place where you worked?" I tried. Maybe he'd answer a direct question. "Where'd you work in 1990?" Normally, two questions in a row are too much for him—he short-circuits and doesn't know which to answer. I ignored my building guilt.

"Church," he responded.

A church? Was this where the rest of the work was hidden?

"Which one?" There are only, like, seven hundred fifty old churches in Boston.

"You know." He waved his hand and looked away. "The one in Copley."

There were at least two churches in Copley Square. A big one, at one end of the park, and a smaller one on the corner of Dartmouth? Clarendon? Whatever. There were churches there. A prickly thrill skittered up my spine. Now, to find out where they were in the church.

The porch door opened. Nini smiled at me. My knees popped as I stood.

"They're having a barbershop quartet in the common room, Joe. Let's go check out the music."

Grumps mumbled something about going to church. My hands got cold. Would he give me away?

"We've already been to church, love," Nini said, releasing the brake on his wheelchair. I relaxed. "Coming, Moxie?"

I quickly evaluated: If I went with them, maybe I could get more info from Grumps, but there'd be no chance of me getting into town until tomorrow.

"I'm gonna pass, thanks." I kissed Nini on the cheek, then leaned over and pecked Grumps too.

The Redhead's right, I thought: I have to go to church after all.

25

I texted Ollie on my way out of Alton Rivers, hoping he'd meet me downtown, but his family was doing some "family fun time" activity on the Boston Harbor Islands. I was on my own . . . which technically meant I wasn't supposed to take the T into Boston. But *tick . . . tick . . . tick*, with Mom at work and Nini busy (not that I would have asked either of them to come with me), I had no other options. It's not as though there was anyone else from school I could ask either—"Hey, let's go hang out in this really dark historical church this afternoon so I can look for stolen art!" Yeah, right. No way.

Taking the risk, I hopped on the Orange Line into Back Bay and walked the two blocks to Copley. The sun beat down, making me glad I hadn't taken my bike. Dehydration on top of rule breaking and yesterday's skinned hands and knees? No, thank you.

Copley Square swarmed with people hanging out, shopping, and sightseeing. Kids splashed in the fountain next to the Tortoise and the Hare statues. The big church sits at the far side of the square, past the statues.

I crossed the park, stopping to buy a lemonade from a cart,

and stood in front of the church. TRINITY CHURCH PARISH FOUNDED 1733, THIS BUILDING CONSTRUCTED 1877 was printed in neat letters on the blue sign. Made from stone and red tile, the church's large arched entrance and big columns don't look like any other church that I've seen—more like a fairy-tale castle. It's also one of the few historic buildings in town I'd never been in. I had no idea that Grumps worked on this.

I chugged the rest of the lemonade, wincing at the brain freeze it left behind, and stepped under an arch into cool shade. I heaved one of the big wooden doors open—

And was staring at a building filled with people, many of whom were turned in my direction, and a couple getting married on the altar.

"Crap!" I whispered, and tried to close the door quietly. But it was on one of those "safety is silence" arms that don't allow slamming. Face burning, I stepped out of people's line of sight and watched the door slowly inch closed. I sat on the steps. Of *course* the church would be in use on Sunday! The other one, across from the square, would probably also be holding some sort of service.

Epic Moxie fail, I chided myself. I came in alone, without researching the churches or even double-checking the photo album. This was the complete . . . antithesis of the logical way I'd figured out where the sketches were. It wasn't even worth pulling out the proof. I was wasting valuable time that The Redhead was probably using to her advantage.

The Redhead . . . she'd been following me for a few days;

that much was obvious. I squinted into the chaotic scene in Copley Square. She was probably out there somewhere, waiting for me to leave so *she* could scope out the church. And she had the luxury of no curfew, no rules about traveling into the city on her own, and no compunction about breaking the law. And I'd just led her to the next hiding place.

Head cradled in my arms, I squinched my eyes shut as tight as I could and willed all of this to go away.

I sat like that until the big doors behind me opened for the bride and groom to exit. The wedding guests trailed behind them like untied shoelaces.

The church was empty! Well, almost. But everyone would be paying attention to what was going on *outside*, not inside. Mood improved, I skirted the edge of the guests and slipped in through one of the big doors.

Inside, the church was massive. Religious murals were painted on the ceiling and walls, and the stained-glass windows sent colorful splotches of light dancing on the pews and floor. It was way, way bigger than the church Nini took me to in our neighborhood, but had the same incense-and-dust smell. I had no idea even where to look for the art. Did churches have storerooms like the state house? Was there a closet somewhere that Grumps had repaired?

As I thought, I walked around the edge of the room, ducking to glance under pews or behind columns. I offered an apologetic smile to two older, straggling wedding guests.

Hopefully they thought I was looking for something I'd left behind during the ceremony.

For its beautiful design and peaceful vibe, all the church was giving me was frustration. Let's face it—Ollie is good at finding stuff; I'm good at figuring stuff out. But I didn't even have a clue to work with. Even though I was sure I'd led The Redhead straight to the next batch of art, I had to admit defeat. It was nearly four, and I had to get home before my mom used her super-sense to figure out that I'd zipped into town on my own.

I took one last glance around the beautiful inside of the building before stepping into the summer heat and sunshine. The bright light after the dim church made me squint, and I wondered, as I crossed the square, if the flash of red that I caught out of the corner of my eye was my imagination.

I sure hoped so.

26

"*You* are in big trouble, missy!"

Her voice cut through traffic noise and Aerosmith, currently playing through my earbuds, and I nearly fell off my bike in shock.

I was at a stoplight just a couple blocks from our house, and after frantically swiveling my head in all directions to figure out where her voice had come from, I spotted Mom two cars behind me.

Crap. What had she seen? The telltale white cords of my earbuds? Another bike-riding infraction? As the light changed, I did a quick inventory—helmet on, nothing obstructing my reflectors, I'd used hand signals all the way back from the T station, where I'd . . .

Oh no.

Mom was coming from the wrong direction! The funeral parlor was in West Roxbury, a totally different neighborhood. Unless she'd been at the supermarket or running an errand or something, she wouldn't come home this way.

My stomach dropped, and I focused on pedaling the rest

of the way to the house, conscious, the whole time, of Mom keeping right with my bike.

She turned into the driveway, and as I straddled the bike outside our gate, I had a moment when I thought, *Just keep going.* Sully Cupcakes and The Redhead won't know where to find you, and Mom won't be able to kill you. But Mom would probably track me down with the intensity that I was using to find the Gardner art.

I waited for her on the porch. She clomped up the stairs, still in her work clothes, carrying a bag from the kitchen store down the street from the T station. That explained it.

"I saw you," she said. I held the door open for her and she brushed past me, not stopping at Nini's like usual. This was Mom at Class-A Flaming Mad—single-minded, focused only on the target of her wrath. Best not to say anything until asked a direct question. I followed her up the stairs as quietly as I could, trying to calm the anxiety in my chest. What had she seen? If it was me coming out of the T station, it was all over. We went into the kitchen.

"I saw you come out of Forest Hills like it was the most natural thing in the world. Alone," she said. "Alone! What were you doing?" She rummaged through the cabinets for a glass, pouring herself an iced tea.

I opened and closed my mouth, unsure of how to answer. Typically, I try to tell the truth. Lying makes my mother go absolutely mental, and I'd rather deal with her fury at what I actually did as opposed to the absolute nuttery that results when I lie, then she finds out the truth. It's like double the nightmare. I never understood why she got all crazy like that about fibs, but now—after finding this stuff out about Grumps—it made sense.

"I went into the Back Bay," I responded, carefully picking my words. "Ollie's family had plans, and I stopped by Alton Rivers to see Grumps, and he mentioned something about working on Trinity Church, so I thought I'd check it out." Not exactly a *lie*.

She held out her hand. "Do you have the card that came with your T pass?" I dug through my wallet, trying to resign myself to the fact that I was about to be grounded until I died (which, considering how things were going, might be sooner rather than later, anyway). I found the printed paper and she pointed to rule #1: Travel to Boston/Harvard Square with a peer.

"Can you read that to me?" she asked, voice even.

I read it.

"Do you understand what it means?"

I nodded.

"So why did you go alone?"

I shrugged. "I told you. I talked to Grumps. He mentioned the church in Copley. I had nothing better to do, so I thought I'd check it out. I know you didn't want me to go alone. I'm sorry. I thought since it was daytime, it'd be okay."

"What if you got hurt? Or lost? Jeez, Moxie, you need to be more responsible. How can I trust you if you take advantage of the freedom you're given?" She slumped into a chair, the anger washed out of her, and took a long swallow of her drink.

For a moment, seeing her like that, I wanted to confess—everything. Let a grown-up handle it. But that couldn't happen. Bad enough that The Redhead was following *me* around and threatening Grumps, I couldn't deal with having something happen to Mom or Nini. Or, just as bad—having Mom decide to pack up and leave for New Hampshire and pull me away from Nini and Grumps for good. So I bit my lip and didn't say anything else.

"Hand it over." Mom extended her hand, palm up.

For a second, I honestly didn't know what she meant—the art?—and then I realized: My T pass. My freedom.

I gulped, and slid it from its spot in my wallet. As soon as it touched her palm, she made it disappear into a pocket. Then she picked up my laptop and stuck it into its zippered case.

"How long?" I asked.

She raised her eyes to me. "Until I decide that you fully understand how serious this business is."

Heart heavy, I nodded.

"This business" was more serious than she knew.

How stupid was I? I blitzed into town not even thinking that I'd get caught, and now I was stuck with no computer, no options, and a handful of days before . . . well, whatever was going to happen. I put "Seasons of Wither" on repeat, and in a dramatic moment threw myself across my bed, prepared to spend the rest of my short life depressed.

Instead, I scraped my face on the corner of the photo album sticking out from under my pillow. I flipped onto my back, hand on my cheek, blood warm between my fingers, and cursed. Steven Tyler sang about how "sadly" he felt for me. I cursed again—this time at him.

The bathroom mirror revealed the damage: a thin red scratch stretching from the left side of my nose, across my left cheek, to the corner of my jaw. Ruby beads of blood lined the trail; some smeared from when I'd grabbed my face. I groaned, then wiped it with a cold washcloth and smeared antibacterial ointment all over it.

With my hands, knees, and now face all damaged, I looked more like an ultimate fighter than a detective.

I grabbed a wad of toilet paper in case the scratch opened up again, and went back to my room.

Desire for more drama depleted, I climbed onto the bed and propped the photo album on my knees. *May as well make the most of my jail time*, I thought.

I opened the book to the page where Ollie and I had found the image of the state house and kept going from there. Even though the photos were of Grumps at his work sites, a certain shirt or a way that his head was tilted would remind me of something that happened when I was younger: like my first trip to Fenway Park or my eighth birthday—when Nini insisted on baking me a cake and put so much salt in it, it was too disgusting to eat, but Grumps devoured a big piece anyway, because he didn't want her to feel bad.

That was the Grumps I knew—the guy who loved my Nini, took me into town, and tried to make everyone feel good.

This lying, sneaking Grumps? He was a total stranger.

I put my head back against the headboard and let the tears come. They ran out of the corners of my eyes and dripped into my hair. It wasn't fair—one of the people I loved most in the whole world had hurt me in a way I hadn't thought possible, and I couldn't even *talk* to him about it, let alone get mad and fight with him over it. Stupid Alzheimer's. Taking my grandfather, his secrets, and—I was realizing more and more—the trust I had in the people around me.

A salty tear stung my scratched face. I swiped it away, along with other thoughts about Grumps. If I was ever going to get through this, I had to focus.

I pulled my proof out of my pocket and spread it next to me. Where in Trinity Church—if they were in that building—was the rest of the art?

I flipped through a few more pages, and then I spotted it— Grumps standing on the stairs of Trinity. I could tell that's where he was because the corner of the blue sign poked into the shot. My heart rate shot up as I pulled the photo off the sticky paper, but even before I turned it over, I knew something was wrong. There was snow in the picture—a lot of it.

January 1990.

January?! The heist was in March. Could he have hidden

the art there if he wasn't working on the building? I doubted it. And the snow on the ground, well, it's not like you could fake that. Especially not in 1990. Was Photoshop even around back then? So why would he lie to me? *How* could he lie, especially with the Alzheimer's?

He's been lying for a long time, Moxie.

The voice in my head was my mother's, but I knew it was right. Grumps had trained himself to lie, over and over again, to protect the things he hid. And he hadn't realized it was me he was speaking to this morning—he thought I was my mom at first—which could also have made him less interested in telling the truth.

But it still hurt.

I put the photo back in its spot and doodled an elaborate question mark on a sticky note.

On the next page, I hit the jackpot. Grumps in front of Old North Church, near Faneuil Hall. Date?

March 1990.

I pulled the picture out so quickly I almost tore it, and added *Old North Church—possible second site* to my proof. But this time, although I was excited, I made myself go through the rest of the album, just in case there were other March photos.

On the second-to-last page, I stopped. There was Grumps, standing in front of an unmistakable Boston landmark. Even if I *hadn't* been searching for millions of dollars worth of stolen art, I would have pulled this photo out for a closer look— it was that awesome.

Grumps stood on a patch of brownish-green grass, left hand in his pocket, a grin to knock his ears off. A green wall, painted with white grid lines and the numbers 2 and 3, was behind him. I didn't even need a second to know what *that* was:

The Green Monster—Fenway Park's famous left-field landmark.

And on the back?

March 1990.

27

I texted Ollie that I had news that was too big for texting—he had to call me as soon as he could—and then I switched "Seasons of Wither" to "Mamma Kin."

From downstairs, my mother yelled, "Oh thank *GOD*."

Guess the fifteen repetitions were getting to her?

Twenty minutes later, my phone rang. "I found two more!" I chattered, and without giving Ollie time to say anything, I launched into my latest discoveries.

"Well?" I said, when I was finished. I admit it—I was a little out of breath from freaking out. "What do you think?"

Instead of a response, all I got was silence. "Ollie?" I asked. I pulled the phone away from my ear and checked the display. It was his number.

"Ollie? You sleepin'?"

This time, instead of silence, I got a low, awful chuckle. A blood-freezing, stomach-dropping, maybe-wet-your-pants-a-little chuckle. A chuckle that grew into a full-blown cackle.

A redheaded cackle.

I dropped the phone like it was covered with bees and raced to the bathroom.

Where I puked my guts up.

When I was done heaving, I rested back on my heels.

What had happened to Ollie? How did The Redhead get his phone? Was he okay? How could I get to those places before her? How could I get *anywhere* while I was grounded?

Sweet chocolate bunnies, I'd lost *everything*.

Another wave of nausea, and I yurked again.

"Moxie?" my mom called up the stairs. "You okay?"

I wiped my mouth and splashed water on my face with shaky hands. The scratch was an electric line on my pasty cheek. I called out some garbled answer to get Mom off my back, and trudged to my room. I had to get in touch with Ollie. My stomach felt hollow and tight, and even though my room was hot, I was cold all over.

I rang his family's landline, but got no answer—just his parents' answering machine, with LeeLee singing "Twinkle, Twinkle Little Star" on the message. I hung up. My next urge was to IM him—but Mom had taken my laptop.

Had The Redhead kidnapped Ollie? Should I call the police? Tell my mom? How had she gotten his phone? Would she hurt him? And, on top of all those questions: *How could I have been so stupid as to blurt out everything without making sure it was Ollie on the other end?* I should have checked first. Every so often his mom or dad called me from his cell—it doesn't happen often, but sometimes, if he puts the phone down and goes out caching, they text to tell me not to expect to hear from him for a while.

Curled in a ball on my bed, the worry ate at me. How

would I know he was safe? Should I call his phone back? What if she answered? What if she didn't?

I was way out of my league. I wished—harder than I'd wished for anything in my life—I wished that I could talk to Grumps.

But the simple truth was that I was alone, and I had to figure out how to deal with this on my own. That made me want to yurk again, but I couldn't. *Get it together*, Moxie, I thought. *Put on your big-girl pants and deal.*

A knock at my door.

"Can I come in?" Mom called.

I grunted.

The door swung in and Mom's eyes went wide when she saw me.

"Moxie! Are you okay? You don't look good." She sat on the edge of my bed and did the patented Mom Test for Fever: a hand across the forehead and a studious frown. "You're clammy and pale. And what happened to your face?"

"Just a scratch," I mumbled, hoping she wouldn't notice that I didn't answer her other question.

She leaned back and studied me. "I think you're coming down with something. We're staying in tonight. I'll call Richard."

Holy close call, Batman! I'd completely forgotten that Mom, Putrid Richard, and I were supposed to have dinner to discuss that "important issue." And, as grateful as I was to get out of dinner—because, let's face it, Putrid Richard could wreck my life just as easily as The Redhead or this mystery—

it didn't take a math genius to calculate that there was a much higher probability of me getting to the bottom of what happened to Ollie if Mom ate with Richard alone.

"You don't have to stay home because of me. I'm sure I feel sick from riding around in the heat and not really eating much today. I'll be fine."

Mom gave me a critical eye. "Riding your bike in the middle of the summer without eating? That's a recipe for disaster." The stuff she didn't say? *Moxie, you have an appetite the size of Rhode Island. Since when do you not eat?*

"Yeah. Dumb move. But I got caught up and just realized that I skipped lunch. I'm sure I'll be fine after I have some water and eat something." And find my best friend.

Mom slid off the bed and stood, eyes narrowed. "Come down and I'll make you something."

I told her I'd be down in a few. When she left, I flopped back on my pillow, still feeling gross. I'm sure she thought I made myself sick on purpose to get out of seeing her and Putrid Richard, but what could I do? Tell her the truth? I nearly laughed out loud at the thought.

The photo album was still next to my bed. As I bent to pick it up, another thought crossed my mind: As the lies I told piled higher, Grumps and I were becoming alike in ways I never expected.

Stressed and jittery, I choked down the dry toast and gallon of lemonade that Mom forced on me before leaving for dinner. Nini was downstairs, watching the Red Sox lose to

the Orioles (her cries of "Criminy! It's the *Orioles*! *Come on!*"
came up through the living room floor every so often). I hadn't
figured out a plan yet, and unfortunately, when I flung my
cell phone to the ground after The Redhead's witchy cackle,
something must've come loose inside—static burst from the
speaker when I turned it back on, and my screen now showed
a starburst of pixels instead of caller ID or texts. Awesome.

At least I could still call out. I dialed Ollie's parents' landline again, but I got their machine and hung up. What kind
of message would I leave? "Um, I was wondering if Ollie had
been kidnapped or anything? Can you have him call me if he's
still around? Did I just ruin our summers forever because I
got Ollie kidnapped?" Yeah . . . negatory.

I had to find Ollie. Maybe The Redhead would be so
excited to have the locations, she'd let him go?

Doubtful. The Redhead wouldn't release Ollie until she
had the art—not just the locations.

And on the heels of that thought—Ollie had the sketches!
Would she figure that out? Try to get it out of him? A pan-
icky sensation tightened my chest.

Focus, Moxie. I had to believe that The Redhead wouldn't
hurt him; that all she was focused on was the art. Maybe by
now she had scoured the Old North Church. As for Fenway, well, that would be tough for even her to get into. And
depending on the schedule . . .

I ran down to Nini's apartment and let myself in. Her
favorite TV chair was empty, but she was standing in front

of the set, hands clenched and face red, Sox hat turned inside out—"rally cap" mode.

It was only the fourth inning, the Sox were down by seven, and by the looks of the brawl on the field, it was going to be a long night. And they were at home. Relief.

She glanced at me. "That headhunter of a pitcher just fired one straight at our best chance for an MVP! He had to hit the dirt to avoid having that face of his rearranged. They're up by *seven*! Who does that?! Everyone's getting kicked out after this mess. How are you feeling, dear?"

At least something was going my way today. There was no way Sully Cupcakes or The Redhead would be able to get into the park tonight. Maybe I could get Ollie back and still beat her to some of the art. I tried not to grin. "Better, thanks. Just wanted to see what all the yelling was about."

Eyes on the TV, she shook her head slowly. "You don't want to see this, trust me." NESN, the local sports network, cut to commercial as the umps finished clearing the field. She turned to me.

"It was a bad day today." I didn't have to ask what she was talking about. I just nodded. She stepped back and sank into her chair.

"Tomorrow will be better," I said.

She gave me a watery smile. We both knew that the number of bad days were creeping up, and soon the good ones would be the rarities.

"Is it okay if I visit more often this summer? I want to find out about where he worked." Asking the question made me feel awkward and shy. I wasn't sure why I felt like I needed permission to go see my grandfather, but on the other hand, it also felt like the right thing to do—a courtesy to Nini, I guess. I hadn't even expected to say that—it just popped into my head and, as a result, popped out of my mouth.

"You can go as much as you want," she answered, surprise all over her face. "*Never* feel like you need my permission to see him, Moxie. He'll love talking to you about that album."

Her words were so gentle, after the day that I'd had, that my eyes filled with tears.

"Thanks, Nini." I gave her a hug. On television, the game was back, teams on their respective benches, and a new pitcher for the Orioles was warming up. I decided to be bold.

"Grumps was talking about churches today," I began, "while you were clearing the dishes. What did he do at the Old North Church?" For a second, I swore Nini's eyes sharpened.

"Oh, I don't quite recall," she said. She faced the TV instead of me. "Something to do with the stairs, maybe? Or perhaps the floorboards?"

Nini was totally lying to me. I knew it, and I was pretty sure she knew I knew it. What else did she know?

"Cool. I'll let you get to the game."

I love my family like crazy, and I couldn't let anything—or anyone—hurt them, Ollie included. No matter how much they lied. That meant one thing: finding Ollie first, then the art.

"Hey, Nini," I added as I was leaving, "are the Sox home the rest of the week?"

And as Nini responded, I thought, Watch out, Redhead. I am going to bring it.

Back upstairs, I paced in my room. I had to get to Ollie's house, to see if he was there. That had to be my first stop when I could get out of my house. Next, I pored through everything I could find about Old North Church in the guidebook Putrid Richard gave me. I even considered sneaking out and trying to find the art myself, but if I got caught—especially after getting grounded earlier that afternoon—I may as well call Sully Cupcakes and ask him to put me out of my misery.

Instead, I made some notes about the church and tried to figure out where Grumps would have hid stuff, feeling completely helpless without a computer. I never realized how much I relied on it for information.

And I needed to find Ollie.

28

After another near-sleepless night, waiting for Mom to leave for work the next morning was excruciating. I dialed Ollie's landline again, and again hung up on the machine. Mom finally took off at ten, my laptop peeping out from the top of her work bag, full of stern warnings not to leave the house.

I only felt a little guilty about that.

Next, I headed down to Nini's apartment. She knew I was grounded, but also thought I was sick.

"I'm not going to visit Grumps today," she said. She felt my forehead. "You look terrible. I think I should be here."

"You have to go," I said, desperate for her to leave. It never occurred to me that she'd skip a visit to ARC. "I'll be fine."

She stared me down. "You don't have anything up your sleeve, do you?" This was her way of addressing my grounding.

"No, ma'am," I answered, trying Ollie's tactic for sweet-talking adults. I smiled. "The only plan I have is for a nap."

She kept her gray eyes on mine. I tried to look tired, yet innocent. Finally, she relented.

"Just a quick visit. I'll be back in time for lunch."

"Grumps will be psyched," I said. And so was I.

Nini came upstairs twice before she left, both times to check on me. I stayed in my pajamas, on the couch, some stupid reality TV show on, trying to be patient. Then I watched at the upstairs window until her car went around the corner. I hurriedly changed out of my pajamas.

I had just about an hour.

Leaving my bike, I grabbed my skateboard and zoomed to Ollie's. His house, a few streets over from mine, was quiet. No cars in the driveway—what did that mean? Were they at the police station? Had The Redhead scared his family into leaving town? I settled behind a tree across the street and watched for a few minutes, staking it out.

Nothing moved. There was no one moving past the windows, no one came to the door, nada. Just as I was about to cross and open their gate, a white delivery truck rumbled past. The driver parked in front of the Truongs' house.

My heart pounded. In the movies, delivery trucks usually contain bombs. Or body parts.

The driver got out, a white envelope tucked under his arm. He opened the gate and climbed the front porch. He rang the bell. Once, twice.

I held my breath.

No answer.

The driver waited for a minute, punched a few buttons on

his handheld computer, and then returned to his truck, taking the package with him.

I exhaled. If it were a bomb or body part, it wouldn't require a signature, right?

My nerves were shot. Clearly, there was no one at the house, and I had to get home before Nini. Giving another long look at the house, I hopped on my skateboard, heart heavy.

Where was Ollie?

5 DAYS LEFT

29

I'd made it home and back into pj's before Nini returned, and that was the end of my free time for the day. She came upstairs with me until my mom came home, and then Mom stuck to me like gum on a T seat for the rest of the night. I managed to sneak in another couple of calls to Ollie's land-line, but again: no answer.

No word from Ollie, no computer, no way to look for the art . . . I was slowly going insane.

I spent another restless night, fighting nightmares.

Thankfully, Mom left for work early, and Nini had a doc-tor's appointment. This time, instead of going to Ollie's first, I beelined for the local library—and its public-access computers.

I had a plan.

Once settled at the machine, I did a quick search on Old North Church. I printed out a list of recent renovations, and even found a blueprint of the building. These I stashed away for later. Next, I tried to launch the IM program I use, to contact Ollie.

An "access denied" message popped up. Confused, I tried it again.

Same message.

I was in the main reading room, not the children's room—where there's never access to sites or software that can be potentially dangerous.

I tried it one more time.

Same message.

A college-aged girl, sitting at the terminal next to me, must have heard my muttered curses.

"Look," she said, pointing above my monitor.

There, in bold letters, a sign stated: ACCESS TO PARTICULAR SOCIAL MEDIA SITES AND SOFTWARE IS BLOCKED DURING PEAK LIBRARY HOURS. PLEASE BE CONSIDERATE OF FELLOW PATRONS AND LIMIT COMPUTER USAGE TO NECESSARY COMMUNICATION.

I fought the urge to bang my head against the monitor. If my communication wasn't necessary, what was?

Frustrated, I signed in to my e-mail program. Ollie and I never used e-mail—we had too many other, faster, ways of being in touch—but I shot him one anyway, wording it carefully because his e-mail pushed to his phone. The Redhead would be able to see it.

Call me ASAP, I wrote.

I didn't know what else to say.

I signed off and headed home, detouring past Ollie's house—which was just as silent as the day before. I was pushing the limits of safety, and I knew it, but I hoped that something had changed.

On my way home, I had a realization: To find Ollie, I had to get The Redhead's attention. To get The Redhead's attention, I had to find more art.

Grounded or not, time to check out Old North Church.

4 DAYS LEFT

30

Time was slipping through my fingers, and I desperately needed to know what was going on with Ollie. I was barely eating or sleeping. I looked terrible, and Nini was convinced I had the flu. Finally, though, I caught a break: a two-funeral day. (So morbid, isn't it?) Mom would be out till late, and this was my only shot.

Nini kept her eye on me all day, insisting I rest on her couch, but once the Sox game started, I was able to make my escape.

Finally!

Upstairs, I did my best to get decked out as Stealth-Moxie Ninja: black T-shirt, denim skirt, black tights (okay, there were a bunch of holes in the pair that showed my Day-Glo legs, but whatever), sneaks. I tossed a flashlight, map of downtown Boston, the guidebook Putrid Richard had given me, a screwdriver, pair of scissors, the crippled cell phone, which Mom had returned since she'd be out late, a crumpled wad of singles I dredged up from my as-yet un-emptied school bag, and two granola bars in a bike sack, and crept to the front door.

And then I turned around. Mom had confiscated my T pass.

For a few seconds, I debated: Do I search her room for it, or use what little cash I had to pay the round-trip fare? If Mom came home and noticed it was gone, I'd be double-dead.

But I also needed a way to get into town. I had to find the art and use it to find out what happened to Ollie.

I blew out a big huff of air. I'd do a quick check in her room, see if I spotted it, and if not—use the cash.

I pushed the door open. Mom's room was immaculate, as always: bed perfectly made, a couple of books on the night-stand, and her trinket box in the middle of her dresser. Even though she wasn't home, I tiptoed in. As carefully as I'd handled the Degas sketch, I grasped the trinket box and lifted its lid. Right on top of her few pieces of jewelry: my Charlie card. I snagged it and stuck it in my pocket, replaced the box, and bolted out of there like security cameras were watching my every move.

Time check: I could still make it back before Mom came home from work. Just in case, I shut off everything in my room and tried to stuff and rumple the bed. Maybe if she looked in on me, she'd think I was asleep.

Not likely, but it gave me a little peace of mind, okay?

I opened the front door, Nini's cheers—the Sox were making a comeback, evidently—following me. She was so into the game, a herd of kids could sneak out and she'd never notice.

Once I was on my bike, coasting through the purple dusk toward Forest Hills, I thought about Ollie again. I even cruised by his house—everything was dark and his parents' cars were gone. I hoped that he was okay; he had to be. Anything else . . . well, I wasn't going to go there. Just the edges of that thought kept my new anger at Sully Cupcakes on a low boil. How *dare* they do this to me? How dare they mess with everything I cared about?

On the train, to get my mind off Sully Cupcakes, I read and reread the entry on the Old North Church in the guidebook. Since Ollie wasn't there to help me strategize, it was the best I could do.

By the time I got off the Orange Line at Haymarket, I was more under control. It was hard, but I tried to pay attention to what was around me more than how I felt. The Redhead had followed me before, and just because she had this information didn't mean she was going to stop. Nothing looked suspicious . . . but in the crowd of a summer night downtown, it was hard to keep track of faces.

Old North Church is at the end of Salem Street in the North End, right near where we'd celebrated mine and Ollie's graduation dinner . . . had that only been a little more than a week ago? Walking past all the restaurants, the smell of sauce and garlic wafting onto the street and the warm buttery aromas from Mike's Pastry Shop made my mouth water. Maybe my appetite was coming back?

Anyway, the church is at the end of the street. It's made famous by Paul Revere—it's where he hung the lights during that whole "one if by land, two if by sea, British are coming" Revolutionary War thing.

Of course, it was closed. I'd expected that, though. A few

couples sat on the front stoop, eating cannolis and laughing. I slipped around the side of the building, eyes moving across the shadows, hoping I wouldn't get caught or spot The Redhead, and proceeded to press on the windows. Old churches in my neighborhood don't have air-conditioning; maybe this one was no different?

The second window in the line spun like a secret-passage-blocking bookcase on *Scooby-Doo. Disco!*

Since it spun on a pin or something right in the middle, even when all the way "open," the window was too narrow for an adult to squeeze through. But a slightly undersized almost–high school freshman? No problem. I carefully lowered my bag into the room, then hoisted myself onto the sill and slipped in.

Instead of having straight-across pews like in a regular church, Old North's seats are sectioned by wooden boxes. According to the guidebook, in the 1700s, high-class people didn't want to sit too close to people who didn't have as much money as them, so they "bought" the boxes and each family had their own reserved seating. Nini had said that Grumps worked "on the stairs or floorboards." Yeah, right. Again, thanks to the guidebook and my research, I learned that "recent renovations" to the church included refurbishment of the gallery seating, the windows, and "repointing" of the brick exterior—whatever that was.

My hope was that Grumps had been the one to do the work on the gallery. Windows and brick weren't his thing.

I went toward the front of the church, keeping my flashlight beam pointed at the ground, trying not to feel the fear creeping up my spine.

A sign pointed to the gallery—up a flight of stairs. My eyes had started to adjust to the semi-darkness, so I clicked off the light and slowly crept to the second floor. Here, instead of boxes, the pews were more bench-like, but still were separated by high walls. The church-goers' backs were parallel to the outside, so they basically were looking down at the middle of the church instead of directly at the altar.

There were dozens of pews, not to mention floorboards and perfectly clean white walls. How was I going to find Grumps's hiding spot? I wished Ollie were with me—he would spot the tiny things I missed—and for the zillionth time wondered what had happened to him.

Focus, Moxie.

I put my "think like a criminal" hat on. There was no place to hide anything up here, unless Grumps put the art underneath the floor of the pews—in which case, I'd never find it. How could I move every bench?

I sat on one of the hard, old benches to think, knowing I was wasting time, but I had to be logical. I had to make this one count. *Had* to.

Ollie's voice in my head said, *See things that are right in front of you, Moxie.*

My eyes roamed the gallery. Straight-backed pews, white walls, floor. Straight-backed pews, white walls, floor. Straight-backed pews . . .

And then I saw it. Once I did, I couldn't believe I'd missed it. In the other gallery, opposite where I sat, there was a bench with a slightly higher back than the others.

As fast as I dared, I scooted around the perimeter of the balcony. My palms were sweating like crazy. Every step I took, I thought someone was going to turn the lights on and yell for the police, or—even worse—The Redhead would reach out from under a pew and grab my ankle.

No wonder detectives and superheroes have sidekicks, I thought. This business is way too scary alone.

I made it to the off-sized pew with no problems—other than my quadrillion near-nervous breakdowns. And once I was there, it was obvious that the back of the seat was higher than the ones around it. Noticeably higher. I ran my fingers over the edge. Same dark stained wood that trimmed the others. Same pure white paint . . . just, about two inches higher than the rest. How had no one noticed this before?

I took a step back and figured it out. The pews were in two rows—like movie theater seats. This one had a pillar in front of it and was near the end of the row.

But that didn't reveal how to get the art out. I dropped to my knees and took out my flashlight. The backs of the other pews stopped an inch or two above the floor, but not this one. It went all the way to the bottom. I had to hand it to Grumps: His carpenter skills were amazeballs. There was no seam, nothing to show that this seat hadn't been built this way in 1723.

I stood and went to the front of the pew, where you'd sit. Then I dropped to the floor and slid under it on my belly.

Again, no cracks, seams, or visible hinges. What would Ollie do if this were a cache? I wished I'd paid more attention when he hid and found stuff.

Think, Moxie. Think!

Logically, I knew that the paintings had to be inside the back. It was the right height to hold the art—about as tall as me. I knocked on the pew. It had a funny, muffled, echo-y sound to it. I knocked on the seat above my head. It had more of a flat tone. The back of the bench was hollow. I closed my eyes and envisioned all the steps on my proof.

The paintings were big, and some of them were on wood.

You can't roll them up, or the paint will flake off and ruin them.

If you couldn't roll them up, and at least one was on wood, there was no way I could get them out from the bottom of the pew. I slid out and stood on tiptoe to get another look at the trim on the back of the seat. Holding my flashlight close, I scanned the entire edge.

And there it was: a seam. A hair-thin line that bisected the wood.

And it was covered in what seemed like three inches of shiny lacquer, stain, or varnish. My poor excuse for finger-nails scrabbled at it, but couldn't catch hold. I rummaged through my bag for the screwdriver. Heavy and cold in my hand, it made me pause.

Moxie, you are about to vandalize a 299-year-old building. A building that is a national landmark and Big-Time Historical Important Place.

A place that's hiding millions of dollars of stolen art, plus the key to the safety of my family, Grumps, and—now—my best friend.

Without another pause, I gripped the handle of the screwdriver like I was holding a knife in a horror movie, and jabbed it straight at the seam. The varnish cracked and turned white, and the flat edge of the screwdriver stuck into the wood like a knife going into a Halloween pumpkin. I wrenched it free and stabbed again. This time, the varnish gave and the screwdriver slid all the way into the seam. I pushed the handle forward, trying to pry the piece of wood up. The popping, snapping noise of the paint and trim separating seemed as loud as a bomb exploding, but there was no way I was going to stop.

Power through, Mox.

A second later, the wood came off entirely, clattering to the floor and catching me by surprise. The screwdriver slammed down, sandwiching my hand between it and the back of the pew. I'd put a lot of power behind that shove, and my hand killed. I stuffed the screwdriver into the bag and shook my fingers, then I directed the flashlight beam into the cubby built into the back of the pew.

There they were: ragged edges of canvas, and, deeper into the cubby—which was barely two inches wide—the edge of a piece of wood.

My breath caught in my chest. Finding the etchings had been amazing, but this . . . *this* was the real deal. These were the pieces that had gotten the most attention. *These* belonged in those empty frames that captivated everyone who went to the Gardner. I blew out a big burst of air.

I tucked the flashlight between my shoulder and ear, so I could work hands-free. Using just my thumbs and forefingers, I gently, gently grabbed the rough edge of one of the canvases and slid it up as high as I could reach.

The weak beam of light revealed blue-black clouds that looked ready to boil off the canvas. The mast of a ship . . . a piece of sail . . . the terrified men hanging on to the boat.

I was holding *The Storm on the Sea of Galilee*, Rembrandt's only seascape.

In my hands.

The flashlight picked up the whirls and strokes of the brush, the shiny whatever-it-was he used to seal it. A few flakes of paint fluttered into the cubby.

How many people had walked by them? Sat here? Leaned against this bench?

I couldn't tear my eyes away. Even though I was way too short to pull the whole thing out, I finally got why people were so entranced by this piece of art—art in general. The painting was like a capsule that collected and concentrated the strength of nature in storm clouds and rough waters. I wished Ollie were here to share this with me, wished we could have another mini-celebration like we had in the state house storeroom. Instead, I completely identified with the terrified apostles on the boat, tossed on a giant sea and waiting for rescue. I blinked away tears.

Finally, I gently replaced the painting, cringing as flakes of paint fluttered into the hiding place, and pulled out another—

Vermeer's *The Concert*. It was even more awesome than the picture I'd seen online: the checkered floor, the woman about to sing, the man with his back to the audience—all of them looked like they were ready to jump off the canvas and perform. Then another Rembrandt, and—too far in for my short arms to reach—the wood panel that the missing landscape was painted on. Five pieces. These, plus the six we'd found in the state house . . .

That meant the ku and the flagpole thingy were at Fenway Park.

Reluctantly, I put the piece of trim back and covered the art. The wood was so mangled—varnish cracked, paint chips all over the floor—as soon as anyone came up to the gallery tomorrow—or later tonight—they'd notice it.

Of course The Redhead would be back, even if she had been here for hours earlier. As high as I was after seeing the art, that reality brought me right down. I couldn't carry it out of here. I couldn't hide it in a better location in the church. And with Ollie probably tied to a chair somewhere, I couldn't take a lot of risks either. I needed it as a bargaining chip, but I hadn't realized that I couldn't move it or keep it safe.

There was only one option left.

I plopped down in the pew and said a prayer, hoping Grumps and Nini and Mom would forgive me, turning my broken cell phone over and over in my hands.

God, if you're listening, please let this be the right decision.

And then I dialed 911.

31

"911 operator, please state your emergency." The voice was crisp and businesslike. Calm.

"I've found five of the missing pieces of art stolen from the Gardner Museum in 1990." I tried to keep my voice even, but it broke a little at the end.

"Say again?" Not businesslike anymore. I repeated myself.

"Is this some kind of joke?"

"No. They're in the gallery of the Old North Church in Boston, left side facing the altar, in a cubby built into the back of a pew. Trust me, you won't miss it. But get someone here, quick. They won't be here in the morning."

Or in an hour. Or twenty minutes. Or who knew when....

The operator asked another question, but I've seen enough cop shows to know that when you call, they trace you. I hung up, hoping she didn't think I was some kid playing a joke, hoping that she had some idea as to the importance of what I'd just told her, hoping that she'd actually get the police or FBI here and not ruin things even more.

I wished I could see them find the art, but it was too risky. And anyway, with the screen busted on my cell, I had no idea what time it was—but knew I was *way* past pushing my luck sneaking in without Mom noticing. I offered another prayer for the safety of the paintings and my family (it seemed like the right thing to do while in church), stood, and slipped out of the pew.

I should've been praying for my own safety.

The Redhead was leaning against the door to the stairwell.

32

I suppose I shouldn't have been as surprised as I was, but I yelped and jumped when I saw her. Had she heard my phone call? Seen me find the paintings? Where was Ollie? I tried to get it together.

Breathe, Moxie.

We were about six feet apart; one set of pews between us. She stood perfectly still, legs crossed at the ankle, back against the door frame, blocking the only exit. Same leather jacket, dark pants, and boots that I'd seen her in for two weeks. Her hair was pulled back, though—Redhead Stealth Mode?—accenting her pointy chin and catlike eyes.

I was *not* going to talk first.

We stared at each other for what felt like twenty minutes. She finally broke the silence.

"Little late for you to be out alone, isn't it?"

I shrugged, hoping that I looked more calm and collected on the outside than I felt on the inside, where my stomach was a washing machine on spin cycle. "And that's your business?"

That predatory grin slid across her face.

"Of course it is, sweetheart," she purred. She straightened, then laced her fingers together and stretched her arms over her head. Her knuckles cracked, loud pops in the silent church. A clichéd thug move on her part, but still, my heart sped up.

"What do you have for us? Sully is getting . . ." She paused. "Anxious. And we both know that the art is here, don't we?" As she spoke, she reached into her jacket pocket. I flinched, thinking she had a gun, but she withdrew a cell phone instead.

A cell phone with a totally recognizable map of the world case.

Ollie's cell.

I swallowed hard, fighting fear and anger. What had this psycho done to him? Also, a shred of my brain held on to her question: Maybe she hadn't seen the mess behind me yet; maybe she didn't know where the art was. Or that I'd called the police.

"Tell me where my friend is, and I'll tell you where the art is," I tried. Deals like that always work in books and movies, right?

"Your friend?" She cocked her head at me. "Oh, the pudgy, sneezy one?" She shrugged, mimicking me from earlier. "I have no idea."

"Then I have no idea where the art is." I crossed my arms. How could I get out of this? And where was stupid 911, anyway? Shouldn't there have been sirens and police cars outside by now?

A little muscle in the side of her jaw twitched.

"We both know that's not true. Tell me."

"I think I've told you enough already today," I responded. "Tell *me* where Ollie is." Hello, standoff.

"Where he is won't matter if you don't give Sully what he wants." The cell disappeared into her pocket. She stepped forward. "I'll just have to get it myself."

The answer was in my hands. I raised my bike bag, which was easily big enough to hold the flagpole topper and ku, not to mention the sketches.

"Not if I don't give *them* to you." As soon as I got the words out I dropped to the floor, barely noticing the sparkles of pain on my skinned knees, and slid under the nearest pew.

Instead of roaring or yelling or swearing—all things I expected—The Redhead just let loose her bone-freezing cackle.

"Seriously, Moxie? Amateur move. You can stay there all night for all I care. I don't have to chase you because there's only one way out."

While she was speaking I inched back, pushing with the heels of my hands, silently slipping from one pew to the next. If I remembered the layout of the gallery, there was an open window on my right, about halfway down the row. Too high to jump from, but it might help me scare The Redhead.

When I gauged that I was at the right point, I took a deep breath, rolled out from under the seat, and hopped up. If The Redhead, at the other end of the room, was surprised that I'd crossed so much floor space, she didn't show it. She just raised her head and looked at me as though I were an insect pinned in a museum case.

In two steps I was at the window. They were huge—almost touching the ceiling—and the bottom panels opened to let in air. Not big enough for a body to squeeze through, but perfectly sized for my bike bag.

Holding the bag by the straps, I stuck my arm out the window, dangling it like you'd hold a toy over a cat's head. *That* got The Redhead's attention. She went rigid, like an electric shock passed through her, and took two huge steps in my direction before I could even react.

"Come closer and I drop it," I growled. "And you don't want the oldest artifact from the museum to end up in pieces all over Salem Street, do you?"

She froze. I was betting that she hadn't done her research—the ku is made of bronze, so even if it *were* in the bag, it would dent and (maybe) crack, but wouldn't shatter (at least I didn't *think* metal could shatter)—and it seemed I was right. She was afraid it would break.

And finally—sirens coming toward the North End.

"Where's Ollie?"

She brushed off the question like she was swatting a fly. "If you drop that bag, Sully Cupcakes won't waste any time, or care that you're a kid, or show you any mercy. You don't want that. And there's nothing I can do to stop him."

"Not like you'd try, anyway," I sneered.

She shrugged for the bazillionth time. "I'm not feeling very inclined to at the moment. Give me the bag," she said, and called me a name that I'd used for Jolie Pearson many times. I was under her skin, for sure.

The sirens were closer. I didn't want to be here when the cavalry arrived. I shook the strap. "Let me leave, and you get the bag."

She cocked her head, considering my offer. I pulled it halfway back into the room, fished around inside, and snagged my keys, cash, and busted cell phone. Stuffing them in my pocket, I noticed a latch on the window frame. Quickly, I looped the bag's strap over it, letting it hang over the alley at the end of Salem Street. The Redhead had stayed where she was. I put my hands up, palms out, in a "surrender" gesture.

"All yours. You take the outside aisle, I get the inside"— we'd keep the double row of pews between us this way—"and you get the bag and the stuff in it. Deal?"

She gave a curt nod. The sirens were outside the front of the church now, and although she couldn't be sure why they were there, I didn't think she wanted to spend any more time in the building either.

I hit the deck again and rolled under both sets of pews. When I got to my feet, I booked it toward the door, seeing a flash of red hair out of the corner of my eye heading the other way. I was on the staircase when I heard her furious squeal. I bounced down the stairs, jumping over two or three at a time, her footsteps pounding above me, and took a flying leap about five steps from the bottom. I crashed into a table holding flyers and meeting notices, pain flaring across my hip, but I didn't stop. The Redhead was halfway down the flight, fury twisting her features.

I raced into the main part of the church, hoping to make it

to the open window, and as my sneakers squeaked against the hardwood floor, a deep pounding came from the main doors.

"Boston police! Open up!"

I didn't stop, but The Redhead's footfalls paused for an instant.

Two feet away from the window, I jumped, reaching for the sill.

Got it! Score!

I heaved my body through the opening and dove headfirst into the alley, landing hard on my side and adding a fresh scrape to my arm and leg—tights even more torn. But I was on my feet in a flash, racing through the alley toward the back of the church, breath burning my lungs. A narrow street to my right. I turned down it and kept running, sweat streaming down my face, until I got to Unity Street, where there were more people. I slowed to a jog, trying to catch my breath, refusing to look behind me, and crossed the Paul Revere Mall to get to Hanover Street, where the crowds were thick and I could hopefully make it back to the T station—and home— in one piece.

Not that it mattered much. After all, The Redhead knew where I lived.

33

By the time I reached the Haymarket T station, my breathing had returned to normal, but I couldn't stop shaking. My arms and legs were jelly-filled bags. And when I finally caught a glimpse of a clock, my heart nearly stopped. It would be close to eleven by the time I got home! The entire ride back to Jamaica Plain, I kept thinking that my escape from The Redhead would mean nothing if my mom killed me as soon as I walked in the door.

When the train stopped at Forest Hills I unlocked my bike and pedaled home, hoping mom wasn't cruising the streets looking for me. At our house, Nini's lights were off, but that didn't mean anything. She sometimes watched the Sox post-game coverage in her bedroom, falling asleep to the analysts' discussion of every pitch. Upstairs, the living room light in our apartment was on; Mom's car was in the driveway. A small splash of relief hit me—if they knew I'd snuck out, the whole house would be lit up and Mom would be frantically calling my cell. I locked my bike to the back porch, then addressed sneaking in.

The stairs were not going to happen. Even if Mom had

fallen asleep on the couch watching TV, it was too danger-ous—I'd have to open the door, creep past the living room, and then make it up the (very) creaky steps to the third floor. My luck would never hold. But the longer I stood outside, the more danger I was in—The Redhead would want revenge.

Seeing my bike locked to the porch railing gave me an idea. I climbed onto the rail, balancing like a dirt-covered circus performer, and found that if I stretched I could just reach the edge of the porch roof. Muscles still aching, and silently hoping I had something left in me to pull this off, I hopped, reached, and grabbed the roof with both hands. The shingles were rough and still warm from the day's heat.

For a moment, I just hung, too tired to pull myself up. Then I swung my legs back and forth, used the corner post to kick myself up and over, and I was on the roof.

Our porch roof sticks out from the back of the house, and it's nearly flat. The problem is that my mom's bedroom and her bathroom window look out over it. I kept low and crawled to the blank wall between the windows. I'd never been up here before, and was surprised at the stickiness of the shin-gles. They made crackly sucking sounds under my sneakers.

I had to get to the third floor. There was a tree outside my bathroom window, and it looked like I might be able to climb up, scoot out along the branch, and get in that way. I'd left it open, but the screen was on it.

Time for the big-girl pants, Moxie.

I pushed through the leaves and branches that crowded the porch to get as close to the trunk as possible. I stepped onto a sturdy branch, and after a few arm-heres, leg-heres, I was even with the bathroom window. The branches were thinner at this height, and I worried they wouldn't hold my weight. As it was, the treetop swayed in the slightest breeze. I took a deep breath, legs straddling the branch, and slid toward the window. The branch dipped. I gasped and tried not to look down.

It held. Gripping the branch as tightly as I could with one hand, I leaned forward, stretched out the other, and barely touched the screen. I needed to get closer.

A scootch or two more, and I was there. The branch dipped and swayed like a boat on a rough sea—an image of the Rembrandt flashed through my mind—instead of a stuck-in-the-ground immoveable piece of nature. Mouth dry, I leaned forward again. I touched the screen, no problem. There were grooves at the bottom of the frame, and I slid my fingers in to raise it. It squeaked, but slid right open.

Disco.

Hands on the sill, another heave-ho and I was off the branch, body half in, half out of the bathroom. My feet clacked against the side of the house. I pushed myself in, pulling a leg over the sill, bent double, and stepped on the toilet seat. A second later, I was through.

I'll be honest: I collapsed on top of the toilet for a little while. My body was exhausted to a degree that I'd never experienced before. I seriously fought falling asleep in the bathroom.

Finally, I managed to stand up, close and lock the window,

and brush my teeth. I thought I'd looked bad this morning. Now, with my hair matted with sweat, wide eyes rimmed with dark circles, face pale, and scratch scabbed, I looked like "death warmed over," as my mother would say.

Seeing as she worked in a funeral parlor, she would know.

I cleaned the fresh scrapes on my arms and legs and finished getting ready for bed. Just as I opened the door to the hallway, my mother's sleep-muzzed voice floated up the stairs.

"Mox . . . Dat you?"

"Yeah," I called. *Please don't come up here, please don't come up here . . .*

"Feel better?"

I mumbled something in reply and headed straight to my room. Tights buried in the garbage, sleep shirt and shorts on, I dove under the covers. *Please don't come up here, please don't come up here . . .*

But she didn't.

And although my body hurt all over, and all I wanted to do was close my eyes, I couldn't stop thinking about what had happened at the church. Had the police found the paintings? What would that mean for Ollie? Would The Redhead take her fury out on him?

And I realized that by placing that 911 call, The Redhead and Sully Cupcakes knew that I had no intention of handing over the art.

And that meant *everyone* in my family was in big-time danger.

3 DAYS LEFT

34

I'm not sure when I fell asleep, but my dreams were awful—Ollie, Mom, Grumps, and Nini were trapped in a deep hole, and I was trying to get them out using the roll of green twine. However, my arms were so tired, I'd pull one halfway up, then let go. They'd tumble to the bottom, and I'd try the next person . . . over and over again.

And when I woke up, I realized that the tiny army with ball-peen hammers had returned. This time, I was in pain even staying still. My calves throbbed, my shoulders ached, hip burned, and there was a constant thrumming in my neck. It got worse when I moved. My shoulders screamed just getting out of bed.

At least I'd only suffer for three more days.

I limped downstairs. Mom had left a note—she'd gone to work—to call when I got up. I poured a glass of juice, returned my Charlie card to her trinket box, grabbed our landline receiver, and dialed Ollie's parents' number.

Machine. Again. I sat at the table, struggling with what to do next—call the police? tell my mom?—and then I remembered:

I *had* called the police—with the location of the Gardner art!

Mom had taken the newspaper, so I flipped the TV on to see if there was a report about it being returned.

Nada.

I'd need to check the Internet, but my computer was still in lockdown and I was too tired and discouraged to sneak another trip to the library. Instead I called Mom.

"Slattery and O'Toole's Funeral Home," she answered.

"Hey, Mom."

"How are you feeling? Any better today?"

I considered my response. If I told her I wasn't better, she'd be more concerned and keep a tighter eye on me. On the other hand, if I told her I *was*, I could get roped into that dinner with Richard.

"I'm achy."

She made a concerned mom-noise, asked if I had a fever, told me to take two painkillers and check in with Nini.

"Since he hasn't been able to get you out of the house, Richard is coming over tonight," she added before I hung up. "He really wants to talk to you. Us."

"Okay," I answered. I was glad she recommended the painkillers, because I was definitely going to need them.

"And I left you a present on my bed," she said.

A present? I hung up and went back into her room . . . and found my laptop. *Disco!*

I opened my computer to check on Ollie and the Gardner art story. Immediately, my IM alert went off—someone had been trying to reach me. I clicked on it, and saw that I'd missed almost a dozen attempts to be reached by Ollie's username, Oxnfree.

A twinge of hope ran through me, but I pushed that down the turnpike. Since The Redhead had his phone, she had his username too—it was all over his text messages.

I checked *The Boston Globe* and *Herald* news sites, but there was no mention of the returned art. I checked the Gardner site too. The return of millions of dollars of art would make front-page news, right? Maybe the police hadn't found it.

Or maybe The Redhead got it out, said a nagging voice in my head.

I went through my filthy laundry from the night before, digging the proof out of my skirt pocket. In the statement column, I added: *Five pieces hidden in Old North Church—all large paintings.* Under reasons, I wrote, *Grumps worked there in 1990. Have seen with own eyes.*

I also added a new statement about the finial and ku being hidden in Fenway Park.

Info up-to-date, I leaned back in my chair to plan. I had to get to Fenway. I had to find the finial and ku. I had to know if the police discovered the paintings.

I pulled on my lower lip. There was one other way I could get some information about the paintings . . . I dialed the number of the Old North Church. It rang. And rang. And rang. According to the website, the office should have been open. Finally, a recorded message came on:

"Thank you for calling Boston's Old North Church, one of

the most significant landmarks in American history. Unfortunately, the church is closed to visitors. Please check back at a later date for tour information. Thank you."

Something's going on, I thought. Although I couldn't be one hundred percent sure that the police found the paintings, *something* had happened to change the daily schedule of the church.

And until I knew exactly what happened, I had to make sure that Grumps, Nini, and Mom stayed safe, and I *really* had to find out what happened to Ollie. I clicked back to my IM window and prepared myself for a log of The Redhead's taunts.

Instead of taunts about Ollie, I saw a list of "You around?" "Hey . . . where are you?" and "Everything okay?" I wanted to believe they were from him, I really did. But over the past twenty-four hours I'd learned that The Redhead would do anything to get what she wanted. I shut off the computer. Seeing "Ollie's" messages gave me an idea.

The phone rang while I was on my way to take a shower. I let our ancient answering machine get it, but lingered at the foot of the stairs to hear the message.

"This is Uniform Connection calling to remind you that a down payment for Margaret Mildred Fleece's uniform is overdue. If payment is not received by the fourth, I will cancel the order."

My stomach dropped. Why hadn't Mom paid for the uniform? Before my brain even finished forming the question, my heart had the answer: *Because she wants you to think that everything's normal until she and Putrid Richard can break the news to you.*

Feeling sick again, I realized that had to be it. Mom wanted to keep things as normal as possible until everything was set.

I showered on autopilot, struggling to forget what I'd heard, then searched for a shirt that would cover an ugly scrape on my arm that came from throwing myself out the church window. No dice. I could hide the one on my leg under tights—and was grateful that the sunset-colored bruise on my hip wouldn't see the light of day—but unless I wanted to wear long sleeves in July (a suspicious wardrobe choice, even for me), I was out of luck. I slapped a Band-Aid over the worst of it and decided not to care what my mom thought, since she obviously didn't care about *me*.

Downstairs, Nini was vacuuming and singing along to her iPod (Mom and I had given it to her last Christmas, loaded with oldies) so I stood in front of her and waved my arms to get her attention. The arm-waving absolutely killed my tortured limbs.

"Oh!" She shut off the vacuum. "You startled me, Moxie. Are you feeling better?"

I nodded. "Just a little achy." She checked my forehead for a fever—I swear, sometimes it's tough having what amounts to two mothers—and asked if I'd taken anything. Once we established that I had fed and medicated myself, I asked her when she was visiting Grumps.

"After lunch. Do you want to come with me?" When I

told her yes, her eyebrows furrowed. "I'm not sure that's a good idea. You could still be contagious." She spoke like I was a germ bomb that would infect all of Alton Rivers.

"I don't have a fever," I pointed out. "I'm sure I'm over it." I crossed my fingers. I *had* to see Grumps, to make sure he was okay. And to tell him I'd found the paintings.

"Let's see how you feel before I go," she said. I knew she hated to tell me to stay home, that she was only trying to protect him—and the other patients. But I couldn't exactly tell her that my "illness" was really from being stressed out, worried, and injured, could I?

I told her I was going to get some air and let her finish vacuuming. My next stop:

Ollie's house.

35

Stepping outside made me jumpy. And, it turned out, with good reason:

Both tires on my bike were slashed flat.

Coldness crept over me. I'd annoyed The Redhead, and even ticked her off with my attitude, but this—this was dangerous angry. She was *pissed*.

And I was her target.

And you know what? I *loved* knowing that I had gotten to her. I grinned.

In case she was watching, I grabbed my skateboard like it had been my first choice and hit the road like it was any other bright, hot summer day. *Take that, Ginger!*

Both his parents' cars were still missing. Had they gone to meet with the police? On TV when a kid was kidnapped, the police camped at the parents' house in case someone called with a ransom request. It had been days with no sign of him—or anyone.

After waiting a while, I stashed my skateboard under a shrub and crossed the street. But instead of heading to the front door, I quietly unlatched the gate and walked around the back for more recon. Unfortunately, most of the windows were too high off the ground for me to peer into; but again, I didn't see anything out of the ordinary.

Turning into a real creeper, Mox, I thought. Again, I was struck by how similar my sneaky behavior was to Grumps's, years ago. I *was* doing this because of him, though, so it was technically his fault.

"Hey! Kid!" a deep voice boomed from a window above me. I jumped about seventeen feet and took off toward the street. Cop, kidnapper, stiff legs . . . it didn't matter. I was outta there.

I fumbled with the latch on the gate and raced to the sidewalk, intent on making it to my wheels.

A door banged open behind me.

"Moxie! *WAIT!*"

That voice was familiar.

"Stop, Moxie! It was a joke!"

I hit the brakes, then spun.

Ollie was standing on his front porch, face red, waving his arms. "Hey!" he yelled.

My achy legs had been replaced by buzzing, adrenaline-fueled ones. That didn't matter, though. They gave out.

I sank to my knees.

36

"You okay? Moxie?" Ollie raced down the stairs to me.

I couldn't believe it. I was so freaked out, I thought it was some kind of trick.

"Is that you?" I asked, dazed. "Where's The Redhead?"

"Of course it's me. And how should I know?" Ollie extended his hand and pulled me up. "Why were you skulking around my house?"

"Where have you been?" I asked, ignoring his question. The longer we stood in the open, the more danger we were in. I grabbed my skateboard and pointed to his house. "Answer me inside."

When the door was closed—and locked—behind us, I asked him again.

"Where have you been?"

"Uhh . . . right here." He blinked behind his glasses in an owly way—totally, honestly puzzled. "What're you talking about?"

I had an Alice in Wonderland moment; reality went fuzzy around the edges. Had I imagined everything?

"Are you a robot?" I tried.

"I think you need something to drink," Ollie said. He left me sitting on the couch and, after some clinking and fridge-opening, came back with two glasses of lemonade. I swallowed half of mine in one gulp.

"Tell me what your deal is," he said. "From the beginning. Wherever that is."

"The Redhead took you. And your phone," I began. I tried to tell the story in logical order, but I couldn't get my brain around it. He listened to my rambling for a minute, then shook his head and cut me off.

"*That's* what happened to it!" he cried.

"What are you talking about?"

"My phone. I went on a Boston Harbor Islands cruise with my parents the other day—which was so awesome, Mox, you wouldn't believe the cool stuff we learned—anyway, on the way back we stopped so I could do a cache downtown. It was one of GI Goh's, a really tough one—" He caught my glare and kept going. "Anyway, my GPS and phone were in the same pocket of my shorts, but when we got home, I only had my GPS. I assumed that I left the phone somewhere, but she must have followed us and took it off a bench or something."

"So she never kidnapped you?"

Ollie shook his head. "I never even *saw* her, Moxie. Of course she didn't kidnap me."

My brain finally caught up with what he was saying. This whole time—*this whole time*—Ollie had been *fine*. I had worried and done stupid things and gave away the location of the art and nearly gotten arrested . . . and he was *fine*.

"I'm going to *kill* you!" I yelled. I smacked him, hard, on the shoulder. He winced. I did it again. "For *days* I've been worried and freaking out and thinking that I had ruined our summer and our lives and going into Boston and getting grounded and you've been *fine?!*" My voice was screechy, but I didn't care. "You *jerk!*"

Ollie backed up, palms in the air. "I tried to get *you*. But when I called your cell, all I got was static. Your mom said you were grounded when I called the landline, so I IM'ed you, but you didn't answer. Didn't you see my messages?"

"I thought The Redhead left them," I mumbled. I remembered her face when I asked her where Ollie was—she hadn't realized that we weren't in touch. *But she certainly played it well*, I thought ruefully.

"But what about your phone? And your parents' cars? I've been calling your landline and coming by here and I never see or get anyone."

"My dad's car has been in for service," he explained. "They're sharing my mom's, so everyone has been leaving super-early. I've been sleeping late," he said sheepishly. "As for the phone, LeeLee plays with the receiver sometimes. She probably shut off the ringer."

The explanation was so simple, I wanted to kill him, I was so relieved.

"I found the paintings and called the police, but I don't know if they have them," I told him miserably. "And I gave her the last location." I was such an idiot.

"*What?*"

Now that I had regained full brain function, I explained what happened.

"Dude!" he breathed. "That's why you're so banged up and a mental mess. What are we going to do now?"

"Figure out how to get into Fenway, I guess. And try not to get killed between now and the Fourth of July." A poor plan, for sure. But now that I knew Ollie was okay, I became totally tired. I wanted to nap and forget I'd ever met The Redhead.

"Don't forget that we have the etching and sketches. Don't worry—I hid them in a safe place." He snapped his fingers. "I nearly forgot—I've got some info for you too. I've been corresponding with GI Goh for the past couple of days—"

"You didn't tell him anything, did you?" Panic tightened my chest.

Ollie gave me a look that would turn a plant black. "Of *course* not. I was discreet. But he gave me some great suggestions for temperate hiding places, and I riffed off his and came up with my own. Since you decided that you're turning the art in, we can call the police and tell them where they are."

I shook my head. The cops were a last resort. I couldn't get the art out of the church by myself and didn't want The Redhead to get her hands on it—which could have happened, though, considering we'd heard nothing of its return—and I didn't want to hand over any more bargaining chips until I was ready. And if I didn't know where the small pieces were, I couldn't tell The Redhead—if it came to that.

"Hang on to them," I said. Making these decisions was

getting easier . . . did that mean I was becoming more and more like Sully Cupcakes and The Redhead?

I left Ollie with strict instructions not to open the door to strangers, get kidnapped, or lose our stolen artwork. We also decided that old-fashioned landline phone calls were the best way to communicate for the time being—once he found the receiver and turned the ringer back on. His e-mail account pushed to his cell, and my cell was only allowing outgoing calls anyway. Couldn't wait to tell Mom that I'd need yet *another* new phone (would that be number three or four this year? I'd lost track).

On the bright side, if we collected the Gardner reward, spending cash on a cell phone wouldn't be that big a deal.

By the time I got home—okay, snuck in the front door, put my skateboard away, and then came down to Nini's apartment—she was getting ready to leave for Alton Rivers.

"Can I go?" I asked. "I'm feeling better."

She felt my forehead. "Hmm. Seems a little warm to me," she said. Why she would say that? I mean, I totally wasn't sick, I'd just . . .

Been out in the sun and skateboarding.

Which Nini couldn't know or I'd get in even bigger trouble for sneaking out while grounded. Awesome.

"Oh. Okay."

"I'm sorry, sweetie," she said. "We just can't take the risk of you bringing something in to the residents. We'll go tomorrow if you're better."

I nodded, miserable. Of course I wanted to see Grumps, but with three days left, I *had* to know where he'd stashed those last two items in Fenway Park.

Oh, yeah, and how to get into the ballpark and find them before The Redhead.

I slumped out of her house and went upstairs. I turned on my Mass Ave Music playlist, flopped on the bed, pulled out the proof, and stared at it.

I had to think like The Redhead. She was probably trying to figure out how to get into Fenway too.

But I had an advantage—I knew what was left. She had no idea what Ollie and I found in the state house, and although she might have *suspected* that the paintings were in the church, unless she was there when they were removed, she really couldn't know for certain.

So maybe I wasn't as bad off as I thought.

I went to my computer. As long as The Redhead didn't know what was left, there was no way for her to determine where the pieces would be hidden. But I could.

A few seconds of Google-fu brought me to a link that summarized all of the changes made to Fenway Park through its history. The most recent team owners had done a lot of work on the ballpark—all since Grumps had hid the finial and ku there. New seating sections—including putting seats on top of the Green Monster, over right field, and other areas of the park—were a major part of it.

If Grumps had hidden the pieces where a lot of construction had happened, there was no hope: Either the pieces had been found and chucked because no one knew what they were, or they were destroyed in the building process.

But there was one area of Fenway that had stayed basically untouched for almost forty years—the Green Monster. It seemed that, since 1975, the actual Monster had been left alone, even though lots of work had gone on *around* it. From watching zillions of games with Nini, I knew that the scoreboard was updated by hand, from inside the wall . . . which meant there had to be some kind of room back there. And Grumps *had* been standing in front of the Monster when the photo was taken.

But until I spoke with Grumps—if he would even tell me anything—I had no way of knowing what part of the park he worked on, for sure. I sure hoped it was the Green Monster.

Hope was all I had left.

37

Holding the sharpest kitchen knife we had, I wondered what would be worse: Cutting the tip of a finger off and spending the night in the emergency room, or getting through this dinner with Putrid Richard?

"How're those cukes coming along, Moxie?" Sir Putrid himself was at my elbow, causing me to jump and almost cut off a finger for real.

"Fine," I said through gritted teeth. I diced the pieces a lot louder than necessary. He and Mom had brought home groceries—plus a "few choice selections" from his garden—and thought it would be fun if all three of us chopped and sautéed and cooked *together*. Gag.

"Glad that you're feeling better," Mom said. She finished seasoning the chicken and handed the tray to Richard to take to the grill. Water bubbled on the stove, and Mom added linguine to it.

I had salad duty.

As soon as Richard's footsteps faded, Mom turned to me, holding an uncooked strand of linguine in front of her like a sword.

"I don't know what your problem is, Moxie, but I'm warning you to lose the attitude. You have been completely sullen and pouty ever since we got home, and it's both embarrassing and annoying. Shape up. I mean it." To make her point, she glared at me after she stopped talking. I dropped my eyes to the counter, resisting the urge to roll them.

"Sorry, Mom, I'll do better" is what I said. What I wanted to say? *Duh, Mom, I'm "sullen and pouty" because Richard wants to move us to New Hampshire soon! Compared to that, going to Boston Classics with Jolie Pearson seems like a treat!*

But I kept my mouth shut and sliced in silence. Then I slid all of the veggies into our biggest bowl, tossed in some lettuce, and carried it to the table . . . but the whole time I was thinking about what Mom said. Did she expect me to get all excited in anticipation of the news that would wreck my life?

Negatory.

Richard returned with a tray of grilled chicken and a big oily spot on his shirt. He caught me staring at it.

"I accidentally tipped the meat tray before I put it on the ledge next to the grill," he explained. "I saw something weird on the ground."

"Something weird?" I tried to sound normal, but could hear the fear in my voice. What had The Redhead done now?

"Yeah! A red squirrel was running up the trunk of that big tree out back. You *never* see them in the city . . ." He went on, but a rush of relief blocked out everything he said (okay, I stopped listening too). To throw my mom a bone, I tried to act excited.

Mom sliced and tossed the chicken with the linguine and sauce, and we sat down to eat. Putrid Richard, wiping his mustache, asked what I'd been doing this summer "thus far."

"Oh, you know . . . solving major art heists, breaking into historical sites after dark, and avoiding mobsters. The usual."

Yeah, I said it.

Mom glared and kicked me under the table. I sighed.

"Hanging out with Ollie and using my T pass a little too much," I tried again. "He and his family just took a cruise of the Boston Harbor Islands that sounded pretty cool." I threw in that last part hoping Richard would go on a tangent of how amazing the islands are. He almost bit too.

"Oh, cool!" he said. "The National Park Service does a lot of work with the group that maintains the islands. We should check them out after . . ." He stuffed a forkful of linguine in his mouth and glanced sideways at my mom. My appetite vanished.

This is it, Moxie. Be cool. I tried to prepare mentally for what I was going to hear—"marriage," "moving," and "soon" were the top three contenders.

"Um, Moxie," he began again. "Your mom and I wanted to talk to you about something."

Stomach tight, mouth dry, I couldn't speak. I just nodded.

Mom grabbed his hand and jumped in. "Richard and I have been discussing something for some time now that involves you. And we didn't want to make a decision without consulting you."

In the past two weeks I'd been scared at least fifty zillion times. But those moments were nothing compared to the terror I felt when she grabbed his hand. I wanted to scream, *Just get it over with! Say it!*

But I kept my mouth shut. I sat on my hands so they wouldn't shake.

"You know how much I love New Hampshire," Richard began. There was a speck of sauce on his mustache. It moved up and down as he spoke. My belly churned and I couldn't take my eyes off that speck. He paused. I guess he was waiting for me to say something, but I couldn't. I jerked out a nod instead.

Here we go . . .

"I'd like to take you and your mom there in two weeks."

Two weeks?! We were leaving in two weeks? That shocker snapped my attention from his mustache. I turned to Mom.

"What? That's so soon!" I cried.

"We've been trying to tell you, honey, but we haven't connected," Mom replied. "We thought you'd be excited."

"Excited? How could you think I'd be excited?! What about Grumps and Nini and . . . and Ollie . . . and—" I hiccupped. Crap. I always hiccup before I cry. "And school?" I couldn't help it, I started crying. It was too much—everything that had gone on with the Gardner art and The Redhead and Ollie and now we were leaving *in two weeks*? Richard and Mom exchanged wide-eyed alarmed glances.

"It's okay," Mom said. "I know you're concerned, but school doesn't start for nearly eight more weeks! This won't make a difference."

"It'll make a difference to *me*!" I cried, blowing my nose in my napkin, hiccupping in full force. Evidently, she *had* been humoring me when I got measured for the uniform. This was way worse than I thought.

"I thought it would be a nice change," Richard said, clearly terrified by my dinnertime snot explosion. "I'm sorry."

"It will be great," Mom said through gritted teeth. "Moxie, you're overreacting."

"Overreacting? Are you serious?!" Hic! "How can you expect me to leave? How can *you* leave?" Hic! "What will Nini do without us? Not to mention Grumps!" If I had any energy left, I would have stormed upstairs, but I was so worn out, I just put my head in my hands and let my tears fall onto my plate while the hiccups shook my body.

"Wait . . . wait a sec," said Richard. "Hold on . . . I think we need a—what do you guys call it, Anne? A time-out?"

"Do-over," said my mother, voice clipped.

"A do-over," Richard said. "Moxie. Moxie, look at me for a second." I shook my head. I didn't want to look at either of them ever again.

"C'mon, Moxie. Seriously. Look at me." Something in his voice made me bring my head up. He gave me an encouraging smile, and slid his napkin across the table to me. I blew my nose on it between hiccups. "I think we have a miscommunication here," he said.

"I don't," I snapped. "You want to take us away from our home. That seems pretty clear to me." Hic!

"I *do* want to take you away," he answered. "On *vacation*."

"Wha-what?" I cocked my head at him and hiccupped again. He nodded.

"Vacation," he said the word slowly and clearly. "That's not what you were thinking, was it?"

I shook my head, unable to speak. They *weren't* getting married. I *wasn't* going to move. All of this anxiety was over a stupid *vacation*.

I was such an idiot.

But the relief was so huge, I didn't care how idiotic I was. It felt as though all the blood had drained out from my arms and legs.

Mom's mouth was wide open. "What did you think? That we were . . . moving there?"

I nodded, and started crying again . . . tears of relief this time. "It's just that . . . that . . ." Hic! "Richard always talks about how much he likes New Hampshire better than Boston, and you didn't pay for my uniform, and I just fih-fih-figured . . ." I trailed off, sobbing. Mom slipped out of her chair and put her arm around me. I turned in to her and cried some more, soaking her shirt and not caring.

"Baby, this is our home. We're not going *anywhere*. For *anyone*. Richard knows that. Right, Richard?"

"Absolutely," he said.

"And I didn't pay for your uniform yet because I was waiting until I got my overtime check from those two wakes I worked last week."

Mom and I stayed like that for a few minutes, until I got

control and my sobs stopped. When just hiccups were left, she straightened and returned to her seat. I shot into the bathroom to clean up. Add a red nose, red-rimmed eyes, and blotchy cheeks to my already banged-up body and scratched face, and you get the idea of what a pretty picture I was.

I went back to the table, feeling a heck of a lot lighter and thinking Richard was a lot less putrid.

"Okay. *Vacation*. Yeah. Sounds great. When do we leave?"

38

It's amazing how a relatively normal night with my mom (minus a major freak-out over a miscommunication) wiped away nearly two weeks of constant stress. I didn't even have any crazy dreams. My life was in a bubble of normalcy.

My bubble burst the next morning, though. Only two days left to find the art. If I made it through the Fourth of July in one piece, Mom, Richard, and I would be heading to the Kangamangus Highway at the end of next week. And knowing it wasn't permanent made me actually look forward to it.

The "making it in one piece" part was key.

I checked in with Ollie, who asked when I was moving as soon as he came on the phone.

"Never," I replied, and explained the misunderstanding.

"So he's Not-so-Putrid Richard now?" he asked, laughing.

"Pretty much," I admitted. "I'm totally lame, I know!"

After a few more minutes of ragging on me, Ollie explained that he'd been doing some research on Fenway Park too— but he'd been studying how we'd get in.

"Doesn't look good, Moxie. The doors to the ticket gates are like giant garage doors that get locked at the end of every game.

There's the players' lot and the ambulance bays, which are where employees park when it's a non-game day, but there's security there if those doors are open. To sneak past them, we'd have to probably climb a fence on Van Ness Street."

I groaned.

"So we're stuck, then?"

"Not necessarily. If we're in this boat, so is The Redhead. Our best bet is to see if we can score tickets to the game on the Fourth and pull a state house."

I considered this. Hiding out in the state house was a huge risk, sure—but Fenway was a whole other (pardon the expression) ball game. There are security guards, Boston police officers, and the zillions of people who work there. I'd been to plenty of games, and seen them on TV, and I knew that emptying the ballpark was serious business. No stragglers.

But we were out of options. And time. I sighed.

"We'll need a *great* plan."

"I'm on it," said Ollie. "People have cached at the park, so I'll see what I can find out."

"Cool. I'm going to talk to Grumps, see if I can get him to lay down where the last two pieces are."

We agreed to check in later, and I headed downstairs.

At least this time Nini agreed that I wasn't a contagious threat to anyone at Alton Rivers. While she got ready to leave, I flipped through the newspaper on her kitchen table, even though I'd checked online this morning. Again, nothing about the paintings. I nibbled a cuticle. The police didn't have them, so The Redhead probably did.

"So I heard you and Richard and your mother are going on vacation soon," Nini said, a mischievous gleam in her eye. She turned onto Centre Street.

I rolled my eyes. "Yes, Nini. We're going on vacation. Not moving." I paused. "You have no idea how much that was stressing me out."

Nini's face softened. "I can imagine. Family is very important to you, Moxie. To all of us. And I really appreciate how supportive you've been of Grumps . . . both before and since he's been in ARC."

Great, now I felt guilty. As much as I loved and wanted to protect Grumps, all I'd been doing lately was betraying him—calling the police, uncovering his secrets, and—I knew this was to come—forcing things to change in a big way.

Luckily, we turned into the parking lot before I could say anything back. Iris was on the phone and she waved us through sign-in. It was another hot day, and the A/C was cranked in the reception area. The rec room? Not so much. Old people get cold really easily, so it's always a slightly drowsy seventy-five in there. Nini stopped to speak with Mrs. Ricci and I went to find Grumps. He wasn't on the porch or in the rec room, so I headed to his room.

The door was closed. I knocked quietly and pushed it open, not wanting to wake him if he was napping. But instead of Grumps lying on the bed, I saw a huge mess: rumpled sheets covered with clothes from his drawers, books in a crooked pile on his end table, and, smack in the middle of it, one hand reaching into his bookshelf—The Redhead. No Grumps.

I was so shocked I couldn't move. Neither could she. We stared at each other for a few seconds, until she sneered and pulled her hand out.

But my shock was immediately replaced with anger. How *dare* she come in here and mess with Grumps's stuff?! *How dare she?!*

I didn't even bother with the "I'm going to act super-cool if you act super-cool" illusion that I'd been cultivating for the past two weeks.

"What the HELL are you doing in my grandfather's room, you freak? Where is he?" I snapped. Grumps's mirror reflected the bright red patches on my cheeks.

She glanced around, probably trying to gauge if there was any way to make it out a different door. Nope. His room has one door, and the windows are small at ARC. Can't have the patients wandering away after dark.

"As if you didn't know," she snarled. Even though she wore her usual "I couldn't care less about you" expression, she was rattled. She was desperate too, if she was checking my grandfather's room in the middle of the day!

Too bad.

I grinned, and took two big steps to reach the side of his bed. Showing her my closed fist, I slammed it into the red EMERGENCY button next to his nightstand. Immediately, an alarm wailed. It'd sound at the nurses' desk and reception—residents used it if they had a medical problem and families used it if a patient managed to wander outside.

"Busted," I said sweetly.

39

Almost before the word finished hitting the air, The Redhead barreled around the bed and shoved me. I crashed into the bedside table, slamming my bruised hip. Everything—water glass, books, Grumps's extra glasses, me—tumbled to the floor. As I gritted my teeth with pain, she took off into the hall.

Seconds later, Angel and two other staffers appeared at Grumps's door with a crash cart and other medical devices.

"What happened?"

"Moxie, are you okay?" Angel helped me up.

I nodded, rubbing my beaten hip, and made a split-second decision: Tell the truth. "Yeah. There was someone messing with Grumps's stuff. I nailed the alarm button and scared her." And, almost as an afterthought, "Where's Grumps? Is he okay?"

"OT," Angel answered. "Your grandmother's with him. The regular occupational therapist is on vacation this week, so we had to juggle schedules." The other staffers left with the medical equipment, but they would return with security. "Who was in here? A shopper?"

Some Alzheimer's patients will wander into other rooms and take something little—an item off a dresser, or a stuffed animal, or a sweater—and bring it to their own room, not really realizing they have it or that it doesn't belong to them. The staff call these patients "shoppers."

"No. Definitely not a shopper. A youngish woman with long red hair." I was getting savage pleasure out of this. Why not turn up the heat on The Redhead? She'd been turning it up on me.

Security showed up a moment later, Nini with them. She clucked and fretted while they questioned me—I gave them a description of The Redhead and told them no, she didn't have a bag or anything with her, and I didn't think she'd taken anything from the room.

Nini, satisfied that I was in one piece and had not been traumatized, turned her attention from me to putting Grumps's things back. She and Angel didn't want him to see his room in such a topsy-turvy state—he was having a good day and the chaos would upset him. So he was playing checkers in the rec room with Mrs. Ricci.

"We'd like to call the police and alert them as to what happened," one of the security guards said. "We can't legally do anything, and need them to act on your information."

Nini, who'd been refolding Grumps's clothes, straightened like a soldier coming to attention.

"That won't be necessary," she said.

"But ma'am," began one of the security officers, "your granddaughter got a great look at her, and perhaps the police could find this person. She might be a known figure in the community."

Nini shook her head firmly, eyes hard. "I'm not putting my granddaughter through that, you understand? Instead, maybe you should revise your security procedures to ensure that no one has access to the facility who doesn't belong here."

You could've sliced and served the tension in the room. Nini stared at the two men until they mumbled something and looked away. Then she went back to being sweet Nini, visiting her husband.

"You haven't even seen him yet, have you, dear?" she asked me.

I shook my head.

"Well, why don't you go find your grandfather and keep him busy while I finish cleaning this mess. I'm sure these fine men have work to get back to, as well." She gave them a meaningful look, and they cleared out. I was right on their heels. Did Nini know something, or was she just protecting family business?

When I found Grumps, he was sitting across from a snoozing Mrs. Ricci, checkerboard still between them, looking out the window. Angel was helping another patient on the other side of the room.

"Hey, Grumps." I pecked him on the cheek when I saw his eyes brighten.

We chitchatted about summer for a minute, and I asked him if he wanted to go outside. He nodded and pointed to the porch. "Go that way," he said.

Angel came over and held the door for me. "Things okay?" he asked. I nodded.

"Yeah. Thanks," I said, shy. It was weird, but I was embarrassed that he was the one who helped me up after The Redhead wrecked Grumps's room. I steered Grumps outside, and Angel closed the door, giving us some privacy.

I plopped into a chair across from him. At first I didn't say anything, just wrestled with what I *should* say. Sully's collection deadline for the Gardner art was one day away, and I needed to keep myself—and my family—safe. Even if "safe" wasn't what Grumps would have wanted, he had to know the truth.

"Grumps, I gotta tell you something that you won't want to hear."

"What is it, Moxie?"

I took a deep breath.

"I broke family rules. I found almost all of the Gardner art, Grumps. Sully Cupcakes came looking for it. He wants it back, and I don't want to give it to him. Tomorrow, I'm going to Fenway for the last two pieces." I stopped, needing to check Grumps's reaction.

He shifted in his chair. "Sully Cupcakes is bad news. This is not safe."

Okay, still with me.

"I know, Grumps. I'm going to give it to the police. But I need to know where you worked at Fenway, so I can get them before Sully Cupcakes does."

He didn't say anything, just picked at a spot on his pants. Was I going to lose him?

"What's in it for me if I help you?"

Slipping a little . . .

"Your family will be safe," I told him. "Sully will go away for a long time." I hoped.

"I didn't want him to have them," he said. "He wanted to trade them for weapons, but I didn't like that. When the statute of limitations is up I'll return them."

So *that's* why he hadn't told Sully! One of the things I'd learned in studying the Gardner case was that now the statute of limitations—the length of time after committing a crime in which you can be prosecuted—expired after twenty years. With Grumps in the nursing home, the paintings would have stayed hidden forever.

"It's up," I said, hoping it would give him some relief. "I'm going to give them back."

He nodded.

"Doing the right thing," he said, "is something I wasn't good at. But I always kept my family safe."

"You sure did," I whispered, holding my breath and fighting the urge to hiccup. "What did you work on at Fenway?"

"The bleachers and the Green Monster."

"Where did you hide the art there?" I pressed him. If it was under the bleachers, we could forget about this right now—they'd be long gone, victims of new construction. It wasn't worth making the trip.

He frowned. "I don't remember."

"Are you sure?"

Grumps knuckled his eyes, as though he was forcing his

brain to show him the location. He shook his head. "I don't know."

This was as good as I was going to get.

I gave him a big hug and kiss. "Thank you, Grumps."

He smiled. "Checkers?"

I went back inside to get the checkerboard, smile still on my face, but innards churning. Getting into Fenway Park would be hard, but getting across the field to check out the Green Monster would be next to impossible.

40

Nini made me promise not to tell my mom what happened in Grumps's room—"We'll keep it inside our gloves" is what she said—but grilled me about The Redhead the entire way home.

"What did she look like?" she asked me for the three thousandth time.

"Nini, I *told* you already—like a redheaded snake," I snapped. "Do you know her or something?" Maybe I could get some much-needed answers on her identity. Until now, I hadn't cared who she was. I mean, if someone is trying to make your life miserable, you don't want to know their favorite color, do you? But now . . . well, we were close to the end. Maybe the more I knew, the better off I'd be.

Nini's eyes remained glued to the road. "No. I have no idea who she is," she said.

Liar.

Nini knew something . . . or, at least, suspected something. Getting her to reveal that info? Next to impossible. But I had to try.

"I don't believe you," I said. There. Bold and Out There.

"Too bad," she retorted. "It's not of your concern. Old neighborhood business."

And that was it. We finished the short ride in silence . . . but Nini had revealed this much: *Both* of my grandparents knew Sully Cupcakes and The Redhead.

After dinner, Ollie called to lay out our final plan.

"Our best bet will be to keep moving after the game ends," he said. "We travel to different sections, duck into the bathrooms after they're cleaned, find anywhere we can to hide until things quiet down."

"Okay," I replied.

"I'm hoping that since they have a double header on the fifth, the crew will clear out fast to catch fireworks."

I doubted it, but I kept that to myself. Ollie had worked hard—even scoring us bleacher seats to the game by trading some Geo-Secret Knowledge—and who was I to burst his bubble? I certainly had nothing better to suggest.

As a matter of fact, I was the one who could potentially ruin the whole thing. I was still grounded, and Mom was off tomorrow. She might decide withholding a Sox game would be the pinnacle of punishment.

"So you wanna hear about what went down in my world today?" I told him about finding The Redhead in Grumps's room, Nini's reaction to the whole thing, and, finally, that Grumps had worked on the Monster.

He whistled through his teeth. "Dude, Mox. This is tough. But we know that The Redhead doesn't have the paintings, or she wouldn't be going through his stuff in broad daylight. She's desperate."

Desperate people do desperate things . . . which worried me.

"What about the sketches?" he asked after a short pause.

"What about them?"

"Well, are we going to bundle up what we have and drop it at the Gardner on the fifth? Call the police once we find the ku and finial? Leave them on a doorstep somewhere? Moxie, we don't even have to *go* to Fenway Park. We can just call and tell them what we know."

I considered his option. Calling the police was so appealing . . . but I didn't have a lot for them to go on—I didn't even know where to look near the Green Monster. Besides, what if the same thing happened that did with Old North Church? How would that keep my family safe? Sully Cupcakes and The Redhead would be furious, and come straight for me.

"We don't even have to call the police," Ollie pointed out. "We could just call Fenway and let their security deal with it."

Now *that* sounded like it would work. Calling the ballpark wouldn't get us in trouble, and it could end the whole thing.

"Let's try it," I said. Ollie did some Google-fu and read the number off to me. I told him I'd hang up and call him back after.

My hands were trembling, but I dialed the phone. After three rings, someone picked up.

"Fenway Park security." The voice was straight out of

Southie—South Boston—an extra thick accent, down to the *paahhk*.

"Um, I'm calling because I think two of the missing pieces of art from the Isabella Stewart Gardner Museum are hidden in the Green Monster." I tried to keep my voice steady, but a few uhs and ums escaped.

"Listen, kid. This ain't no joke line. This is serious stuff—"

"But it's true!" I interrupted.

"Don't make me call the cops on you," he said. Only, with his thick accent, *cops* came out like *cawps* and *you* came out *yuh*. Then he hung up.

Awesome. My insides felt like a deflated balloon. Well, at least we tried.

I called Ollie back and broke the news:

The only choice we had was to get the stuff, turn it in, and get The Redhead caught—all while staying out of the picture.

"We've gotta do it, Ollie. It's the best way to make sure everyone stays safe."

He groaned. "Fine . . . If by *everyone*, you mean me too. I don't want to get not-kidnapped again."

Getting kidnapped would be a picnic if this fell through.

THE LAST DAY:
July 4

41

Squeezing through the crowds of people filling Yawkey Way before a game should be exciting, energizing, and fun . . . not scary, paranoia-inducing, and stressful. People were decked out for the Fourth in crazy getups: Every third person had on oversized star sunglasses, a giant Stars and Stripes hat, or a shimmery wig. Anyone could have been The Redhead. Or Sully Cupcakes, for that matter.

Maybe my rejected disguise idea for the state house wasn't bad . . . it was just for the wrong place.

"I don't even know where to look," Ollie said nervously.

"Me neither." We pushed through the crowd, roasting in the heat, heading around the park to the bleachers entrance.

My mom, surprisingly, had agreed to let me go to the game with Ollie. She even said we could hang out downtown until the fireworks were over—a gift of extra time that I hadn't dared hoped for. I think she was feeling bad about the whole moving/vacation confusion, and wanted to reduce her guilt load. This morning she made me charge my cell phone (I hid the cracked screen from her) and helped me pack a day's worth of provisions: sunscreen, cash, hat, bottle of water, and camera in a lightweight backpack that replaced my bike bag. When she went on to other things, I found a substitute for the screwdriver I'd given The Redhead, and added what was left of the granola bars from the pantry.

We found the entrance for our seats, and let the gray-haired security guy scan our tickets. He did a quick search of my bag too.

"What's this?" He pulled out the screwdriver.

"I have no idea," I said. "Must belong to my grandfather."

"You can't bring this into the park," he said. "Is it senti-mental or functional?"

"Uhhh . . ." What was the right answer? "Functional," I decided. He pitched it into one of those industrial-sized gar-bage cans next to his station.

Ollie shot me a look.

"What if he expected me to come back for it if I said 'sen-timental'?" I told him when we finally got into the concourse. "I didn't know what to do."

"True," he said, glum. "I just hate losing the only tool we brought."

"Let's get to our seats. We've got a while before we have to worry about tools." Although it had been a couple of years since I'd been to a game—the last one was with Grumps and Nini, before Grumps's Alzheimer's had really kicked in—I couldn't get into it. Instead, I was just impatient and antsy. I just wanted to get today over with—however it shook out.

Ollie, though, was Mr. Swivel-head . . . eyes on the concrete concourse, the green painted steel columns, the lines for food, the weird crawl spaces underneath the seats, the vendors selling Sox shirts, key chains, hats, and just about anything else you could imagine. I nudged him.

"What're you looking at?"

"Everything. We'll be invisible once this place empties out."

I grinned.

We followed signs to the bleachers. All the new concession stands and construction underneath the section reinforced my idea that if the finial and ku had been hidden here, they were gone. Or we wouldn't be able to find them without taking the Chilly Dog stand down. As soon as we got to the seats, Ollie pulled out his graph paper and started charting the park and everything we'd passed on our way in.

"Impressive!" I told him.

"Necessary," he muttered.

The bleachers are smack in the middle of center field, and some sections have to be covered with a tarp during day games so the batter can more clearly see the ball. Our seats were closer to right field, a few rows back from the visitors' bullpen.

Despite my stressed-out state, a tiny spark of excitement flared in me once we got settled. It was a perfect New England summer day—electric blue sky, sun blazing—and the park was filling up. We watched the players finishing their stretches and warm-ups and clear the field.

"Ladies and gentlemen, please rise as Boston's best rocker, Steven Tyler from Aerosmith, sings our national anthem."

I admit it—I squealed like Jolie Pearson and jumped out of my seat. I craned my neck to see him on the big screen, but also glimpsed him standing off to the side of home plate, just him and a microphone.

Steven didn't disappoint—he threw in a few trademark wails and ya-ca-ca-ca-cas after "Oh say does that star-spangled banner yet wave . . ." At the end of the song, three military planes flew over the stadium, low and loud. Awesome.

Ollie nudged me. "We may as well enjoy it, huh?"

I nodded.

The Sox took the field and we got comfortable.

When the seventh inning stretch rolled around, I scanned the crowd. The Sox were up, 6–2 over the Jays, and the way the Blue Jays' pitching was going, there was no risk of a loss.

With two outs left in the eighth, I could barely keep still. Ollie nudged me.

"Let's go," he said.

This was part of his plan: Get into the concourse before the stands started emptying, so we could avoid security.

There were a couple of food vendors still open, so we each grabbed a soda and a slice of pizza. Those, and the granola bars were it for the rest of the night. He showed me his map and pointed to our hiding places.

"This way," Ollie said, munching on his slice. He pointed toward the right field box seats. "The wall's lowest there."

We poked around the souvenir tables and watched the

final Blue Jays out on a TV mounted near the women's bathroom (final score: 9–2, Sox). Nini would be psyched. "Dirty Water" played over the loudspeakers, and the crowd started to leave.

Ollie and I followed the herd toward the exit, then doubled back and got into another group heading toward a different gate. My neck and arms were wound with tight cables, and I couldn't even look at Ollie. My face was like a mask—one with a big, frozen "I'm a kid who just went to a baseball game" smile on it, but if I opened my mouth I was afraid I'd yurk.

"Crowd's thinning," Ollie muttered. "Phase two."

We ducked into our respective bathrooms. I closed myself into the farthest stall from the "in" door—Fenway bathrooms have separate entrances and exits. Being alone was even more nerve-racking. What if I got caught?

I also wondered when my mom would start to worry about me. The fireworks were at ten, and she'd know the T would be crowded. Once she decided it was too late, though, she'd get her crazy on. The thought was comforting. No matter what happened tonight, if I was late, my mom would come looking for me.

A couple of times, the bathroom door banged open. I balanced on the toilet seat and waited, heart in my mouth. Twice the visitors flushed and left (ew—*Wash your hands!* I wanted to shout), but the third time the banging door was accompanied by a squeaking noise that must have been a mop bucket. I breathed through my mouth and listened hard.

Okay Moxie, okay . . . I told myself. *They're gonna clean the stalls too.*

Sure enough, a couple of minutes later, I heard the first stall door bang open and a wet mop slop to the floor.

Door number two: *Bang! Slop! Swish!*

I was in the sixth stall. There was an exit door almost diagonally in front of me. I took a deep breath . . .

Bang! Stall door number three opened, as well as number six. Without looking at anything but my escape route, I raced out of the bathroom.

"Stop!" yelled a woman's voice. Heart in my mouth, I pounded through the concourse and headed straight for the dim space under the seats.

I squinched in as tight as I could, totally exposed but in deep shadow, heart slamming so hard, I thought it was going to explode. I held my breath, listening for the woman who yelled at me, but there was no sound. The concrete step-like seat risers from the section above me dug into my back, and my nose stayed inches from the gnarly floor—*how does it get so sticky and filthy when no one walks over here?* I focused on that, instead of the woman in the bathroom, who was probably calling her supervisor about me.

I pulled a knit cap out of my bag and stuffed my low ponytail into it. A few minutes later, the cleaner from the women's bathroom passed by, pushing her squeaky mop bucket in front of her. I died a thousand deaths, hoping she wouldn't see me. But she went by without a word. Some time after that, I spotted another cleaner leaving the men's room.

Ollie and I had agreed to meet in the storage area under box 92—one section over from where I was now. Although I could hear voices and loud noises—clattering/clacking . . . maybe they were cleaning the concession stands?—I didn't see anyone else. Slowly, I scooted along on my scabbed hands and knees, trying to keep to the shadows. I had to cross the access ramp to one of the boxes, which put me totally into the open. I had never felt so exposed, and was convinced Fenway security was going to tackle me the second I stood up.

Finally, I was under section 92—exactly where I was supposed to meet Ollie.

Only Ollie wasn't there.

42

I lay in the crawl space, feeling the panic rise in me like flood waters. At what point should I go look for him? Worst of all was not knowing how much time had passed—I hadn't thought to put on a watch (okay, not that I even *have* a watch to put on . . . but I could've looked for one in my mom's room or something) since my cell phone screen was busted.

From my uncomfortable, filthy spot, I spotted a sliver of light around the edge of the nearest entrance gate's big garage doors. Not that that helped much. It wouldn't get dark until close to 8:30.

Well, I couldn't stay here forever. With or without Ollie, I had to finish this.

Just as I was getting ready to slip out from my hiding spot, a dark blur sprinted across the concourse and slid in across from me.

Ollie.

Our faces were inches apart. The sunburn was beginning to show on his cheeks and—yuck—I could smell his pizza breath. He was panting pretty hard. I hoped he wouldn't sneeze.

"Where were you?" I whispered, relieved. He put his finger over his lips to shush me and shook his head.

He pointed at the access ramp to box 92, then back to himself and to me, and made "running fingers" on the ground between us: We were going to make a break for it.

He held up a closed fist. We listened, but there was no way to tell if the voices that floated on the air were from people on Van Ness Street outside, or in the concourse. He raised his fingers:

One.

I stuck my palms to the ground, under my shoulders, and curled my toes—getting in push-up position.

Two.

Deep breath.

Three.

I sprang up and saw stars—I forgot that the spot we were hiding in had such a low-angled ceiling, and I cracked my head right on the edge of the risers above me. I staggered out from the storage space, not caring if anyone saw me.

Somehow, I kept from crying out, but my eyes watered and vision blurred from the pain. I gritted my teeth and reached around to the back of my head. A blinding flash of hot pain seared across my scalp. I hissed.

"C'mon, Moxie!" Ollie grabbed my hand and tugged me onto the ramp and into the seats. My legs were such jelly, I could barely stand up straight. I collapsed into a second-row aisle seat, not even worrying that we were in the middle of a crazy illegal activity.

I rested my head against the chair in front of me, closed my eyes, and took deep breaths through my mouth. Nausea rippled through me.

"Dude, Moxie," Ollie said, voice low. "I think you took a chunk of concrete off the stadium when you jackrabbitted out of there."

He was trying to make me smile, but the axe-like pain in my head destroyed my sense of humor. My noggin *killed*.

When I didn't respond, he fussed with the zipper on his backpack and rummaged inside. He pressed a bottle of water into my hand, lid off.

Slowly, I tilted my head—the park spun a little, but settled—and took a sip. Two or three sips later, the pain was more manageable and the sensation that I'd fall off the seat if I didn't hang on went away. I finally looked around. The sky was that deep gold of summer before sunset, and shadows reached across the field, darkening home plate and stretching beyond second base.

Fenway during a game is pretty impressive—when it's packed with fans, you can feel the excitement in the air—but when it's empty, well, it's spooky. The seats are folded and silent, the lights out in the press box, the infield covered like a dead person wrapped up . . . I shuddered.

"It's waiting for something," Ollie said.

I nodded, sending new bolts of pain into my head. That was totally it. "Yeah. Like the ghosts of anyone who ever came to a game."

We sat quietly for a minute.

"You okay to move?"

"I think so. Where to next?"

He pointed to right field wall at the seats in front of us. "We climb over, stay right at the edge of the wall, and get into the visitors' bullpen. There's a bathroom in there."

Did he have to go?

"Okay." I gripped the back of the seat in front of me and willed myself not to get dizzy when I stood. It didn't work. The park spun, but settled and held. Ollie's face was concerned.

"I'm okay," I repeated. The back of my head felt funny, though.

I stepped into the aisle, Ollie behind me, and we scooted into the front row. It was less than a four-foot drop from the top of the wall to the warning track. Ollie did it easily, and had I not beaned my brains on a hundred-year-old concrete riser, I would have too. Instead, I sat on the wall, flipped onto my belly, and awkwardly lowered myself to the ground. I was pretty sure that when the right fielder stood there, the ground didn't dip and sway like he was at sea. I kept my right hand against the pads lining the wall and followed Ollie around the perimeter of the outfield.

He reached the bullpen, unlatched the door, and tugged, but it didn't budge.

"Crud!"

"I got it." I reached over the door and fiddled with the *inside* latch. It swung open and we scooted in, then sank against the wall, backs to the outfield, where we hopefully wouldn't be spotted.

Again, I reminded myself. Although it seemed like the cleaner had chosen not to report me.

I brought my fingers to the back of my head, and they sank into a spongy wetness on my cap. When I took them away, they were dark with blood.

Awesome. Bleeding head wound on top of trespassing and all kinds of illegal activity, I thought. I decided not to tell Ollie. But we needed to get out of here, fast.

"Time check?"

He took out his cell phone. "Nearly eight," he said. "Hungry?"

I shook my head, stars of pain dancing across my vision. "Nope. You?"

Instead of responding, he dug into a granola bar. I tilted my head back and closed my eyes.

"Why are you doing this for me, Ols?"

"Doing what?" he asked. Peanut butter and chocolate wafted toward me.

"Breaking and entering. Hiding stolen property. Accessorizing."

"Accessorizing?" He laughed. "I don't think that's what you mean."

"You know what I mean." Throbbing blobs of color floated across my eyelids. I was getting sleepy.

"For my college applications," he responded. I whacked him. He sighed.

"Moxie? Seriously? I'm doing this for the same reasons

you are: Because it's right. Because I love Grumps and I don't want anything to happen to him." He paused. "And because you're my best friend and I'll miss hanging out with you next year and I don't want you to be alone when Sully Cupcakes kills you. Okay?"

"Okay, Ollie." I stifled a yawn.

"MIT is gonna love this," he muttered.

What felt like a second later, Ollie was nudging me. His face was right in mine.

"Moxie? *Moxie?*" His eyes were wide and he looked kind of panicked.

"Wha—what is it?" I winced. More head-hurting.

"You were asleep. It took me a while to wake you."

I guess I had been. It was full night now, no hints of blue or streaks of leftover sunset above us.

We made it.

"Let's do this," I said. I swigged from a water bottle and stood. Luckily, the world stayed still, but the pain behind my eyes thumped with every heartbeat.

"We stick to the edge of the warning track, cross the Green Monster. There's a door at the far side," reviewed Ollie.

I nodded. What we didn't need to say aloud: Once we got in, we'd have no idea where to look.

"On three." This time I counted us off: "One . . . two . . . three!"

Bullpen door open, we slipped into the darkness and deep shadows at the edge of the warning track. Some of the stadium's lights were on, casting a clear glow over the infield, but the light didn't reach us.

I was walking on the field at Fenway! No matter what happened later, this was still pretty darn awesome. Nini would love this . . . it's just too bad I could never tell her.

We'd reached the Green Monster. Up close, the scoreboard was even larger than it seems on TV or from the stands. Each letter was almost as long as my forearm. We had to pass the National League column, all nine inning boxes, plus the lights for outs, strikes, balls, and at bat. Then the door. Crossing it was like being in one of those carnival games where you're supposed to shoot the duck with a water pistol. The ducks float past a painted background and you just fire. That's how exposed I felt. And, to be honest, my feet felt far away from the rest of my body.

The Monster doorknob didn't stick out, probably so a player wouldn't impale himself on it; instead it was a flat twist-ring set into the door. Ollie grabbed it and turned—*please, please let our luck hold*—and it opened.

"Disco," he said, and grinned.

We stepped inside the Monster.

43

Heat and sweat: my first two impressions of the inside of the Green Monster. The smell made me want to yurk. Ollie pulled the door closed behind us, and opened his new cell phone. It let out an icy light.

"Flashlight app," he explained.

"Sweet."

The space was narrow—a concrete wall to our left, the field to our right. Ollie and I could probably stand side by side, hold our arms out, and stretch across the whole area. He flicked a switch, and two bare bulbs sparked to life. We blinked against the brightness. I shut them off again.

"Why'd you do that?" he asked.

"Because our eyes won't be adjusted when we leave," I explained. "What if we have to make a quick exit?"

"True," he said. "Hey—watch out!" He gestured to a large slanted concrete column in front of us. "Wouldn't want you to hit your head."

"Ha-ha. Hey—check this out!" I pointed to the inside wall of the Monster. What I'd thought was graffiti at first was actually the signatures of Red Sox players from past and current teams. Even some left fielders from other teams had signed it!

We took a few minutes to read the names. "Manny Ramirez!" "Ken Griffey Jr.!" "Johnny Damon!"

"Brian Cashman?" said Ollie.

"GM of the Yankees," I explained. "Ick."

"Let's find this thing," he said. "I'm starting to get antsy."

I was too—and my head was still muzzy and painful.

The good thing was that there weren't many places to look. The concrete wall and floor were solid. That left the beams above us. Although a normal-sized adult could probably reach them with no problem, we needed a few inches. And I was in no shape to give Ollie a boost.

"Think they're up there?" Ollie asked.

"No other place they could be, I guess."

He took his phone and we crept farther into the Monster. It was pitch-black at the edges of Ollie's screen. But despite the darkness and my bleeding head wound, I saw something familiar in the corner . . .

"Jackpot!" I called. "Over there." We stepped closer, and I hoped that it would turn out to be what I thought it was.

A stepladder.

It was a short one—Grumps had a similar one that he used for changing lightbulbs or doing work in the house.

I took Ollie's phone, holding the light steady, and he lugged it to the beam closest to the door and set it up.

"What now?" I asked.

"We climb up, check them out, knock on them to see

231

if there's a cubby or something. Hopefully get lucky." He shrugged. "Want to go first?"

"Totally." I'd just be extra-careful.

One, two, three steps up, and I could reach the beams. Unfortunately, when I tilted my head back and lifted my arm to knock on the beam, the world spun again.

"Crikey!" I said. I closed my eyes, and when I reopened them, things had settled.

"You okay?"

"Not really. I need to come down." My head swirled again as I reached the floor.

Ollie watched me carefully before he stepped on the ladder. He climbed up and knocked on the beam in a couple of spots. Definitely metal. He came down, we slid the ladder over, he went up and knocked again. Metal.

We moved to the next beam. And the next. He climbed and knocked four more times. I was getting discouraged. Maybe the last two pieces of Gardner art would stay missing forever. And then . . .

"Oh, hel-lo," I said. Instead of the metal ringing when Ollie rapped on the beam, there came a flat wooden echo.

"Got it!" said Ollie. He ran his hands over it, searching for a seam or hinge. I didn't think we'd be that lucky, and I was right.

"It's here," he said. "There's a crack that looks like part of the beam." He pointed.

"How can you even *see* that?" I asked.

He grinned. "Ollie-vision," he answered. "Do we have anything we can use to pry or break it open?"

I didn't. We explored the Monster some more . . . numbered cards for the scoreboard, an old-school phone, a couple of folding chairs, and a table. That was pretty much it.

"What about these?" I asked. The cards were threaded onto giant rusty nails sticking out of the wall. "Think we can get one loose?"

"One way to find out." Ollie and I tested all of them, and one gave the teensiest bit. We took turns wiggling, twisting, and scraping at the concrete around it using a rock that I found wedged in a corner. After what felt like forever, it came free.

The nail was almost as long as my arm, and heavy. Actually, it was more like a spike than a nail.

Ollie grabbed it and went back up the ladder. I checked his phone: 9:23 p.m. Thirty minutes to the fireworks, maybe ninety before the parents flipped out. But most worrisome was the total *lack* of a sign from The Redhead. At any second I expected her to burst into the Green Monster.

Crack! Ollie slammed the spike into the spot on the side of the fake beam. Paint and wood chips sprinkled down. *Crack!* He did it again. The third time, a hole opened. He reached in and found some kind of latch, and swung the side of the beam open.

He pulled out a shoebox, tucked it under his arm, and came down. Together, we huddled above the white light from his phone and stared at the lid.

"You take it off," I said. "You found them."

Ollie nervously licked his lips and gave a half nod. He lifted the top of the box off, revealing two tissue-wrapped bundles—one of which he handed to me.

Slowly, I unfurled the paper. Cold, dark metal, shaped like an hourglass with a smaller bottom than top . . . I was holding the ku. A three-thousand-year-old vase. My hands started to shake—whether from my nerves or head injury, I didn't know.

Ollie unwrapped the finial—the flagpole topper. An eagle with its wings outstretched; although age had tarnished it, you could still see the bronze in some places.

"Whoa," he breathed.

"Pretty awesome," I agreed. We traded objects, and I traced the feathers on the bottom row of the wings. Then we rewrapped both pieces and stuffed them in the bottom of my backpack. After all, we weren't enjoying them in a museum.

He folded the stepladder and we tucked it against the concrete wall near the door.

"Ready?" he asked.

"Definitely."

He pushed the door open onto the very dark corner of the field.

"Crap! Mox—" he began, and took a step back, hands up.

So *that's* where The Redhead was . . .

44

Without thinking, I grabbed the only thing close by: the stepladder. As Ollie backed into the Monster, I stood to the side of the doorway, just out of The Redhead's sight. Ollie was awesome: His eyes never flickered in my direction, just stayed focused on the woman in front of him. I gripped the ladder as tightly as possible, its edge digging into my palms. When the tip of one black boot stepped over the threshold, I swung it through the open door as hard as I could.

The shock from contact traveled up to my shoulders, and I dropped it onto the warning track.

"Run!" I screamed at Ollie.

We booked it. At least The Redhead had been knocked over by my horrible makeshift weapon. She was rubbing her chin and climbing to her feet. Two steps later and I realized we had a very big problem: On the field, we were done for. We'd have to run too far to reach a spot in the wall where we could climb into the seats. I grabbed Ollie and pointed at the Monster, then I raced back and snagged the ladder with one foot, dragging it close. The ground tilted, but I was determined not to stop.

The Redhead, swearing up a storm, grabbed the other end of the ladder with one hand. I pulled as hard as I could, and her hand came free. Ollie was by my side. Together, we brought the ladder to the door we'd just exited and had now closed.

"Open it!" I shouted. The Redhead lunged for me. Her nails bit into my arm, and she clawed at the strap to my backpack.

"I am out of patience with you," she snarled, and gripped my other arm.

Bad move, Redhead. I whirled my forearms like first Grumps and, later, the self-defense instructor in gym class had drilled into me, breaking her grip. For good measure, I slapped the side of my hand into the front of her neck—another Grumps lesson. She coughed and staggered back. Behind me, Ollie huffed up the aluminum rungs.

Fenway has a ladder that scales the external Green Monster wall. Before the seats were there, grounds crews would retrieve balls caught in the net that stretched across left field, meant to protect cars and people on Lansdowne Street.

"Up!" he wheezed.

I spun and raced to the ladder, head throbbing. Scrabbling up the rungs, I heard The Redhead, breathing ragged, pounding across the grass. Just as I reached above my head, grabbing the rung sticking out of the Green Monster's wall above the scoreboard, I felt her grab the stepladder. I kicked out with both feet, pulling myself up, and raced up the rungs.

Blood pounded in my ears—and I tried not to think about what was coming out of the back of my head. The rungs felt like they went on forever. The Redhead was below me, and I needed as much distance between us as possible. My hands cramped.

And then I was at the top. Ollie yanked on my backpack, helping me over the edge and into the Monster seats. During a game, these are the best seats in the park. I had no interest in the view, but was grateful that the clubs and restaurants on Lansdowne were decorated with miles of neon—their glow made it easier to see, as we were in the shadow of the stadium lights.

I spared a glance over the wall. The Redhead had maybe four rungs to go.

"Let's go!" Ollie pulled me toward the left field bridge. We raced in front of the seats, no longer trying to hide from The Redhead or anyone else. Ollie wheezed like the Little Engine That Could. I hoped his lungs wouldn't give out before he could take a hit from his inhaler.

We reached the bridge, and I slowed. I didn't hear her boots. I dropped behind the seats and snuck a look: She was on her cell phone.

Crikey.

She wasn't alone.

Ollie sucked on his inhaler.

"Go!" I whispered, and we started across the bridge.

In order to activate our exit strategy, we had to get all the way back to the "front" of the ballpark, and get into the players' parking lot. It was a thin plan in perfect conditions, but now? Forget it. We'd never make it.

We crossed into the enclosed concourse outside of the third base luxury boxes. All of the doors were locked. We had no choice but to run straight through. Nowhere to hide.

Ollie asked me to stop, and we squished into a doorway. He took out his phone, fingers flying over the keys as he wheezed.

"You're not calling the police, are you?" I asked. Although, seriously, at this point, it wasn't a bad idea. We were, after all, carrying stolen property and being stalked by a bad guy.

He shook his head but didn't speak. Whatever he was doing, he finished it fast and hit his inhaler.

"Let's go." The hall was empty. We kept going toward home plate, this time at a quieter, slower jog instead of an all-out sprint. No sounds except our own breathing.

That is, until the *shick-shick* of a shotgun.

45

Even if, like me and Ollie, you've never been around a gun, or fired one, or even seen one, you know that sound from movies, video games . . . whatever. And if you hear it in person, it goes through you like an ice needle.

It came from in front of us.

We froze.

And if I hadn't spent nearly two hours in a bathroom, I probably would've peed my pants. Seriously.

The end of the concourse was in deep shadow, but when the boxy-shaped man stepped into view, the only feature I needed to see were his eyes: They made a snake's seem warm.

Sully Cupcakes.

"I want the bag," he said. "And the location of the rest of the art. No messing around. Or I'll shoot your friend." He pointed his gun at Ollie, who immediately started wheezing.

I didn't doubt him for a second. I held my hands palms out, in surrender, and slipped the straps from my backpack off each shoulder. This'd be the second bag I'd lost to the bad guys. I put it on the ground and lightly kicked it in his direction. Doors to three luxury boxes were between him and us, and the bag slid along to about the halfway point, and came to a stop.

He came closer, gun pointed at the ground, picked it up, and unzipped it. I guess the tissue paper blobs satisfied him, because he closed it and slung it over his shoulder (which, considering how big his shoulder was and how ratty and small my backpack was, would have made for a really funny picture . . . in a non-life-threatening situation).

"Where are the other pieces?" The gun was still at his side, but that didn't matter. I couldn't stop looking at it.

Everything I went through to find the pieces, to figure out Grumps's plans, to keep my family safe . . . I mean, I knew I was in danger that whole time, but to actually see Danger, right in front of you, is a whole other piece of cheese. The Redhead, although creepy and annoying and stalker-y, had started to feel benign. She was totally after me, but it never seemed like she was going to *actually* hurt me—just vandalize my property and try to scare me.

This guy? All he needed was a reason. And maybe not even that.

"Pew in Old North Church," I answered, not hesitating. "Gallery level."

"Anything else I should know?"

The etchings. I didn't know where they were. I skated my eyes to Ollie. He was wheezing away, hand clutching his . . . cell phone?

Please don't get me—or you—killed, I thought. Although this was *not* turning out to be the Best Summer Ever, I was starting to appreciate the little things: Like even though I'd have to wear an ugly uniform to Boston Classics, I'd still live long enough to go to high school. Ollie and I could still hang out . . . you know, that stuff.

I shook my head. "That's all I found."

Sully Cupcakes tilted his head, evaluating me. I gulped. My heart was pounding so hard that it made the pain in my head recede a little.

"She's lying, Daddy." The Redhead's patronizing purr came from behind us. "They found something in the state house." I resisted the urge to spin around.

Daddy?! Was this some kind of weird, "we're dating but I'm going to call you Daddy" thing? Or was she actually . . .

"My daughter says you're lying," he said. Well, that explained a lot—crime as a family business. In a different situation, I'd find it ironic and funny. Ollie kept wheezing.

I gulped again. "We found a few pieces, but we left them there. Storeroom under the dome. Third floor. In a dresser."

Sully nodded to The Redhead. "Tie them up," he said. I guess he was satisfied with my answer. "We'll take them down in the elevator."

The Redhead's boots clicked across the floor and she wrenched my arms tightly behind my back. I wasn't going to give her the satisfaction of wincing, so I bit my tongue when she pulled my arms harder than she needed to. The edges of my vision were gray, like they were wrapped in a sweater. The dizziness was back too.

Finished with me, she snapped in my ear, "You are such a

brat," and jerked hard on my wrists. Jagged pain shot to my shoulders, and I sucked air through my teeth. I swear she was smiling when she walked over to Ollie.

"Need . . . my . . . inhaler," he gasped. She let him take one pull off it before tying his arms.

Sully retreated into the shadowy end of the hallway, and The Redhead gestured for us to follow him. I was totally convinced that he was standing just to the side of us in the dark, waiting, ready to kill us on the spot. But that didn't happen.

Instead, the four of us stood in a civilized line, waiting for the elevator.

And when it opened, it was filled with people.

FBI agents and SWAT team, mostly.

ONE WEEK AFTER

After the passing out (me), level-12 emergency-room-necessitating asthma attack (Ollie), and arrest (The Redhead and Sully Cupcakes), came Seeing My Mother in a Cop Car, Getting My Head Stitched Up, and Spending Two Nights in the Hospital. Since then, I've spent a lot of time in Witness Debriefing Room 2A in the FBI building in downtown Boston.

You know what? The vending machines here have lousy snacks.

I've had to tell my story over and over again, to different agents and police officers. It's gotten to the point where I'm tempted to just throw in random details—a biker gang, or a flock of wild turkeys—just for variety. But that would be bad. Ollie's in the same situation, but they have us separated—he's in room 3D. They're checking for inconsistencies in our story.

The only person—besides my mom, of course—who's been with me the whole time? Agent Alan Goh. He's been the lead investigator on the Gardner heist for the past fifteen years.

And when he wasn't running down dead-end leads, he got into another hobby: geocaching.

That GI Goh guy, who Ollie was always competing with? Who gave him "suggestions" on a good, temperate hiding spot for the etchings and sketches?

Yeah. FBI agent.

You never know who you're dealing with online.

It's a good thing Ollie *did* ask for his help. It made Agent Goh suspicious. And when I called 911 about the paintings in the church? They found them, just never released that to the media. Agent Goh was hoping that whoever returned the paintings would hand over the rest of the art. So Agent Goh was the guy who wrangled the Sox tickets for us, gave Ollie some info about security cameras, and generally was letting us do everything while he watched from behind the scenes— which is why it was so easy for us to sneak into Fenway. So when Ollie posted a message about needing an escape route *from* Fenway Park ASAP, Agent Goh called in the cavalry. He had no idea he was dealing with a kid, but he was pretty certain that he was dealing with some high-level stolen property.

Score for Agent Goh.

"So, Margaret—" began the 465th state police officer I'd spoken to this week.

"Moxie," Agent Goh corrected. I gave him an appreciative smile.

"So, Moxie, I think we're done. Thank you for your time." The officer finished his coffee and stood to leave, which was good, because I was seriously wiped out and my headache was back. The doctors told me I'd given myself a "severe" concussion—the equivalent of getting hit by one of the Patriots' linebackers. I told them I was a baseball fan.

"Thank you, officer." My mom stood and shook his hand. The door closed as he left. "Is that all of them?" she directed at Agent Goh, who was in the same spot—head of the table, to my right—that he'd been in every day.

He checked something on his iPad—probably another cache. Although Agent Goh debriefed all day in the room with me, he and Ollie had eaten lunch together a few times, swapping cache sites and techniques. Ollie was psyched to learn that his geo-guru was in law enforcement.

"Yep," he answered. Then, turning to me: "Moxie, you know how grateful we all are to you. Thanks again for your patience. The Gardner Museum would like to thank you and Ollie publicly for your role in all of this."

"Are you sure that's a good idea?" Mom asked.

Agent Goh ran a hand through his spiky dark hair. Sully Cupcakes and The Redhead—whose name, I'd found out, was Fiona—were being held on lots and lots of charges, several of which included kidnapping and endangering children (me and Ollie). They'd never see the light of day again. But that didn't mean everything was okay.

"If I were you, I'd keep my name out of the spotlight," he said. "Moxie is going to be well-protected and perfectly safe, but it's going to get crazier before it gets better."

Tell me about it. The media was covering the story constantly, and although Ollie and I hadn't yet been named as the kids involved—we were too young—it would only be a matter of time before someone spilled who we were. And *that* would make starting high school by myself a freakin' party. Couldn't wait.

But after all that had happened, I knew I could handle it. So could Ollie.

"We had plans to go to New Hampshire next week," Mom said. Ollie's family had decided to send him to Wilderness Scout camp on the Boston Harbor Islands for a couple of weeks until things quieted down. Both of us needed a break.

"Great idea. Do that," said Agent Goh. "I'll let the office up there know where you're staying and give you their number in case you need anything. And Moxie, the DA wanted me to let you know that your proof is going to be entered into evidence for the prosecution."

A small wave of disappointment moved through me. I'd handed the proof over days ago, and I kind of missed it. Agent Goh assured me that I'd get it back after the trial.

I said good-bye and we headed for the elevator.

Mom had driven into town. We had a stop to make on our way home.

As we got in the car, she turned to me. "Doing okay?"

"My head hurts." She gave me a painkiller and I closed my eyes and leaned my forehead against the window.

"Do you think Grumps will be mad at me?" I asked, eyes still closed. "I broke a lot of family rules."

"Grumps will be glad that you are safe and that the art is

where it belongs," she said. "And it's my rules you should be worried about breaking, not his."

I cracked one eye open, but she was smiling. Having her daughter nearly kidnapped or killed by gangsters had made the "You are in so much trouble, young lady" lecture much softer.

"I can't believe you did all that on your own," she said for the thirty thousandth time. "Why didn't you tell me?"

I shrugged. "I wanted to keep you and Nini out of it," I said. "I was afraid you'd get hurt, or be angry, or that something would happen to Grumps." Although, based on Nini's tight-faced expressions since I'd been released from the hospital, my hunch that she knew more than she'd let on was confirmed. She and I would need to have a conversation—soon.

Mom shook her head. "You are just like your grandfather."

"I'll take that as a compliment."

She stopped the car in front of Alton Rivers. "Want me to come with you?" she asked.

"I got it," I said.

I hadn't been to see Grumps since everything went down at Fenway. I was as nervous about this encounter as I had been with Sully Cupcakes. As I crossed the reception area, I took a deep breath.

He wasn't in the rec room, but Angel was. He waved and pointed to the porch.

I opened the door. Grumps was in his wheelchair, facing

the garden. From his posture, I could tell he was alert. He turned when he heard the door close behind me.

"Moxie! I've missed you." I bent down and gave him a big hug.

"Grumps, I have to tell you something," I said. I hiccupped. The tears started.

"You found it all?" he said. I leaned back, shocked that he would remember our conversation from last week. I nodded and wiped my tears.

"Who has it?"

"The museum. Sully is going back to prison."

He bobbed his head, once, like that was all he needed to hear.

"Good, then. It's Wednesday," he said. "I saved you my pudding. Want to play checkers?"

"Sure." I hugged him again, hard, and went to get the board.

AUTHOR'S NOTE

Several years ago, I visited the Isabella Stewart Gardner Museum in Boston and became fascinated by its history and the theft that made the museum famous:

Early in the morning of March 18, 1990, two men dressed as Boston police officers overwhelmed the security guards at the Isabella Stewart Gardner Museum and then spent over an hour alone in the building, stealing thirteen pieces of priceless art. These masterpieces have yet to be found.

The theft simultaneously captures my imagination and breaks my heart: This beautiful artwork, if not preserved or stored properly, will be ruined. Moxie and Ollie's adventure in discovering the pieces is purely fiction—just me, playing detective and coming up with exciting hiding places.

However, I have tried to accurately represent the publicly revealed information about the theft, using the museum's website, public FBI information regarding the missing art, and visits to the museum as my main sources. I've also tried to accurately represent Boston, its neighborhoods, and its landmarks (taking a few minor liberties here and there).

As of this writing, the Gardner theft is still unsolved and under active investigation by the FBI and US Attorney's Office. All parties hope for a safe return of the artwork.

For more information about the theft and the five-million-dollar reward offered by the museum, go to: www.gardnermuseum.org/resources/theft. Your library might have a copy of Ulrich Boser's *The Gardner Heist* (Smithsonian, 2009), or the documentary *Stolen* (Virgil Films), which also detail the events surrounding the robbery.

Who knows . . . maybe you'll be the one to find and return the art!

ACKNOWLEDGMENTS

So many people helped me create this little work of art:

My agent, Sally Harding, who fell in love with Moxie and her grandfather a long time ago;

My editor, Liz Waniewski, who shaped and developed the manuscript with care and thoughtfulness;

My Penguin cover designer Danielle Delaney and publicist Molly Sardella, who make the book look beautiful and help it to reach readers;

My Penguin copyeditor, Regina Castillo, who patiently corrects my grammar mistakes and plotting gaffes (any mistakes left in the manuscript are mine, not hers);

My writing group: Annette, Gary, Heather, Kate, Megan, Phoebe, and Ruthbea, who read draft after draft and offered insight and constructive criticism;

My colleagues, Dr. Kimberlee Cloutier-Blazzard, Leonie Bradbury, and Laura Tonelli, who answered my varied and ignorant art history, curatorial, and restoration questions;

My mom, who read chapters as I finished them, pushed me to write faster, figured out continuity errors, and babysat while I worked;

My crit partner, Jennifer Jabaley, who kept me on track;

My readers, who make my day with every letter or e-mail they take the time to send;

My friends Dianne and Scott, who gave Moxie their Jamaica Plain apartment and left work to photograph the Trinity Church sign;

My friends: Anne, Mike and Wendy, Katie, Kerri, and Shelagh, who support me and listen patiently;

My husband, Frank, who gave me a membership to the Gardner Museum, research materials, and the support, space, and time to write this book.

All of you have my heartfelt thanks and deepest appreciation.

Special thanks to teachers who match books with children; the local libraries and independent book stores like The Book Rack, in Arlington, MA, that enhance our communities; and to readers everywhere.

KEEP READING FOR A
SAMPLE OF THE SEQUEL!

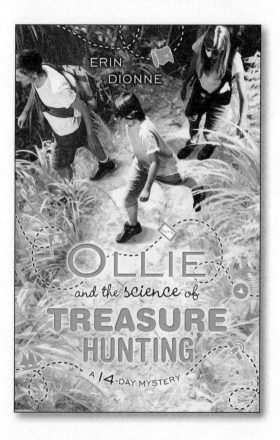

BEFORE

"Stay out of trouble."

Kids hear that all the time, and most of the time we barely pay attention.

But when an FBI agent says it, and it's the fourth time in two weeks that you've been to the federal building in Boston? You listen.

Or try to.

My mom, Agent Goh, and the lawyer who my dad insisted be present after our second trip—but who didn't seem to do anything other than drink more cups of coffee than was humanly possible—were in Conference Room B, the same one I'd been in the other three times I'd been "debriefed." That was a nice way of saying "questioned until I couldn't remember my name anymore."

Agent Goh leaned across the table, his gelled spiky black hair glittering in the overhead light.

"Stay out of trouble for me, okay?" he repeated, but this time with less of an "I'm an FBI agent" serious ring to it and more like the tired way my homeroom teacher last year would say it, when she'd get a headache and pinch the bridge of her nose.

1

"Stay out of trouble, lay low. And have fun." He leaned back in his chair. "Geocache. Hang out by the campfire. Swim." Then he turned his gaze to my mom. "Mrs. Truong, thank you for being so understanding. We believe this is the best course of action for Oliver. It will keep him out of the spotlight and let us wrap up the case against James O'Sullivan."

My mom, whose hands were folded together so tightly the knuckles were white, gave a curt nod, like her neck was wound too tight and it hurt her to move it. "Of course. He loves camp. It just seems so *soon* . . ." She trailed off and took a minute to sweep a stray piece of sandy hair behind her ear. My mom's had the same hairstyle ever since I can remember—and has swept the same piece of hair back forever—but today the gesture revealed how tired she was. And for the four thousandth time since all of this started, I felt bad. I hadn't understood what solving one of the biggest crimes in Boston would do to my family. Everyone was stressed. News vans and reporters had been camped out in front of our house for *days*. This morning, Mom and I had to leave through the back door and cut through our neighbor's yard to get out without them seeing us. My dad had taken two weeks out of work—weeks he'd been saving so we could go to Vietnam and visit my grandmother in the fall. That trip would be rescheduled. Even my little sister, LeeLee, was freaked out. She'd wet the bed three times last week, and she hadn't done that in over a year.

"You're not in any danger, and neither is Ollie," Agent Goh said. "We're confident that Sully and his daughter were working

2

alone. We just need to keep Ollie out of the media spotlight so we can do our jobs. The media glut has been a bit . . . distracting."

Their "jobs" were collecting evidence from the three historical landmarks my best friend, Moxie, and I had broken into or defaced in our quest to find over $500 million in art stolen from the Isabella Stewart Gardner Museum—which we'd found, and returned, and were each $2.5 million richer because of it. Or we would be, when they finished verifying the paintings' authenticity. But thanks to some guy who worked in the restoration department at the museum and had visions of being a TV star, our names had been splashed all over the media—a "distraction" for the FBI, but miserable for me, Moxie, and our families.

Mom sighed, and I felt lower than a snail's butt. Staying out of trouble had always been pretty easy for me. When you're short, a mix of Caucasian/Vietnamese, asthmatic, overweight, and look a little too much like the kid in that animated movie about the old guy who floats his house away with a zillion balloons, there isn't much trouble to get into. I played video games, geocached, and hung out with my friend Moxie—who was already on her way to New Hampshire with her mom and her mom's boyfriend (that was their solution to the "lay low for a couple of weeks" directive).

My parents couldn't get more time off work, so I'd be heading to Wilderness Scout camp on the Boston Harbor islands. My troop was scheduled to go in August, but the FBI wouldn't let me wait that long—so I was going with another troop from Boston, with a bunch of guys I didn't know. Not that I cared much. After spending two weeks either dodging reporters or in Conference Room B, I was ready to get outside and away from this stuff.

Staying out of trouble? No problem.

Riiiighhhht. . . .

WILDERNESS SCOUTS TROOP 7

Harbor Islands Camping Trip Roster—July 18–August 1

Mr. J. Fuentes	Scoutmaster
Dr. A. Gupta	Parent volunteer
Derek Symonds	Troop Leader, 17
Steven Washington	Troop Leader, 17
Peter Mallory	16
Doug Spezzano	16
Jorge Vargas	16
Horatio Fuentes	15
Ravi Gupta	15
Cam Przybylowicz	15
Jack Kadleck	14
Manuel Ramierez	14
Christopher Imprezzi	13
Provo Member: Oliver Truong	13

To: All Troop 7 Scouts attending the BHI Camping Trip

From: Scoutmaster Fuentes

Subject: Orienteering Challenge

To kick off our 2 weeks of summer camp, we're beginning with the annual Orienteering Challenge/Scavenger Hunt. Below are a series of coordinates and clues that you must navigate to find our departure point. Our boat leaves promptly at 2 pm; the challenge begins at 1 pm.

Good luck!

1 pm: Begin at N42 21.60384 W71 3.37272

- Find the statue of someone named Red. What's he holding?
- Cross the Greenway, but instead of an X, these "rings" mark a spot. How many are there, and what is it?
- Who barks at N42 21 32.87 W71 2 58.79?
- Not a rose, but close! We salute you.
- End coordinates: N42.3564864 W -71.049773

DAY 1

1

Here's how you get into trouble trying to find a boat:

Get there first.

"Not a rose, but close . . . Not a rose, but close . . ." I squinted at the clue again. I was standing just past the New England Aquarium, the sea lions in their outdoor tank barking for more tiny fish from the handlers. The first of Scoutmaster Fuentes's riddles were really easy for me to solve: the Red Aubach statue in Faneuil Hall, the Rings Fountain on the Greenway, and the aquarium's sea lions. But the rose one? This was tough.

I closed my eyes, turned the riddle over in my head:

Not a rose, but close.

Where were there roses in Boston?

That's when I realized I was "distracted by the shiny," as Moxie says. Sometimes, when you're trying to find something, it's actually right in front of you—you just can't see it because you're looking at something else bigger and shinier. The word *rose* was a distraction—the crux of the clue was "We salute you." What do we salute?

The flag.

That was it! There was a giant flag in downtown Boston—at *Rowes* Wharf!

I headed down Atlantic Avenue, the aquarium behind me, dodging tourists and people dressed for work, and soon came to the giant rotunda at the Boston Harbor Hotel. The flag that waved in the wind there was taller than my house.

I stood underneath it and typed the final set of coordinates in my handheld GPS, then took off.

The traffic on Atlantic Avenue struggled past, the cars' exhaust adding to the heat of the morning. I swiped my forearm across my brow—a Wilderness Scout no-no; we were supposed to use a handkerchief when in uniform—but the sweat came right back.

The GPS chimed. I glanced down. Direction shift. East.

I turned left, onto the Harbor Walk—this cool paved path that had been built along Boston's waterfront, behind all the hotels, restaurants, and shops. Moxie and I had plans to walk the whole thing this summer, but that hadn't happened.

Most of our summer plans had recently changed.

The GPS chimed again. North.

I turned. Sweat rolled down my back. I'd have a wet patch there when I took my pack off.

Now the water was to my left, a swanky apartment building was on my right. Sweet boats—so sweet they had decks and wooden trim and, from what I could see through the windows, TVs larger than the one in my house—were docked all along the route.

Would I be getting on one of those?

The GPS arrow started blinking, which was how it signaled that I was approaching the destination coordinates. I looked all around. A big boat—really big, like, it had a *helicopter landing pad* on it—was parked in front of me.

Seriously? Wilderness Scout Troop 7 sprang for a yacht?! No way. Not possible.

I was the first person here.

I stopped in front of the yacht. My GPS was blinking like crazy. This *was* the spot.

I checked my watch: Fifteen minutes to spare.

No Wilderness Scout troop could afford a yacht with a heli-pad. What the . . . ?

Then, over the lapping of the water came a cross between a bleat and a honk. It sounded like a sick goose.

I walked down the length of the yacht, toward the harbor. A regular harbor islands ferry bobbed in the water. The horn blatted again.

Typical Boston, I thought. It's a fight over a parking space.

A few bleats later, a very sleepy-looking guy appeared on the deck of the yacht. There was some yelling—apparently the slip was supposed to be empty and ready for the island hopper boat we'd be taking—and then the yacht started rumbling and two other guys materialized to untie it.

"Yeah, baby! That makes six years. In. A. Row!" The shout came from behind me, at the head of the pier. I followed the sound.

A tall, lanky kid with sandy hair, an untucked uniform, and a smug expression leaned against one of the concrete pilings, pack at his feet.

"Hey," I said, sticking out my hand. "I'm Ollie."

He shook it, hard. "Derek. Troop leader. I didn't think any other troops were coming on this trip," he said, gesturing to my Troop 5 patch.

"I'm provo with Troop Seven," I explained.

"Oh. Were you dropped off or somethin'?"

"No," I responded, not understanding what he was getting at. Then it clicked: He thought he'd won the orienteering challenge to find the boat. "I got here first," I said, a prickle of anxiety finding its way into my stomach.

His brow furrowed. "Not possible," he said.

"Uh . . . yeah. It was a good course, though—I nearly got tripped up with the Rowes Wharf clue," I said, hoping this wasn't as big a deal as his scowl made it seem to be.

A dark shadow came over Derek's face, and he stepped away from me. Just then, three other uniformed scouts came around the corner and introduced themselves. One, Steve, had a mess of dreadlocks tied at the nape of his neck and a Troop Leader patch sewn onto the pocket of his uniform. The other two guys were high school age too—one, with broad shoulders and close-cropped hair, introduced himself as Pete, and the other, with dark hair and a pierced ear, was Horatio. All three of them looked a little surprised to see me there.

"D?" Troop leader Steve raised his hand in a celebratory high five. "Six years, right?"

Derek turned to me, eyes hard. "Nah," he said. With an eardrum-busting honk, the yacht unmoored and steered out to sea.

Turn the page to read

THE FIRST TIME MOXIE WAS IN BOX 92, SEAT 13

a short story by Erin Dionne, starring Moxie and Grumps!

THE FIRST TIME MOXIE WAS IN BOX 92, SEAT 13

The big guy with the glasses came up the ramp quick, like he was leaving the park. His little girl, about five, dressed in a pink Sox hat and pink and white jersey, was sad faced and sticky behind him. Chocolate and vanilla ice cream—the soft, swirly kind that came in the dark blue bowls shaped like Red Sox hats—blotted out the "B" and the "O" on her shirt.

They'd just about reached Moxie's aisle seat. The dad stuck his hand into his shirt pocket. Moxie hadn't realized she'd been staring until his shadow stretched over her and blocked the sun.

"Take 'em," he said, holding two stubs out to her. "They're good seats."

Moxie took them, surprised. She knew where the seats were. She'd seen the back of the guy's head ever since she was four, when she'd started coming to games. Grumps told her that the people who had season tickets in their section started to recognize one another after a while. Moxie was eight now, and she knew a bunch of the regulars: There were the five ladies who wore Varitek shirts two rows in front of her and Grumps, a group of three old men behind them who argued all the time, and a few others. But she paid special attention to the big guy because he and his daughter had the best seats in the section: front row.

"Thanks," she said, voice croaking, but he was gone, taking his sticky daughter to the concourse.

"Grumps, we're moving up."

Moxie turned. Grumps had had season tickets for about fifty years, and, he was proud to say, the same seats in the right field box for the last twenty. Moxie was his standing date for all weekend games and any on school holidays. She handed him the stubs as the seventh inning ended, and they wormed down to the seats against the crowd of hot dog buyers and bathroom breakers.

Past Pesky's Pole, Fenway's right field wall dips in, curving into the crowd and creating the weird Right Field Corner that traps ground balls and drives visiting right fielders crazy. There is no row A, B, C, or D in that section—another of the Fenway quirks that Moxie loved. She and Grumps squeezed past the older guys in the first two seats, then a teenaged girl and guy, then came to the empty plastic chairs: Row E, seats 13 and 14. A big, sticky puddle of ice cream flooded the concrete in front of her seat, the dark blue plastic Red Sox cap/bowl floating in the middle of it. Screwed to the wall was a sign: DO NOT INTERFERE WITH BALLS IN PLAY. GROUNDS FOR IMMEDIATE REMOVAL FROM THE PARK. A graffiti artist had added "YOU IDIOT" to it with a black magic marker.

Moxie couldn't believe the difference a few rows made: She could hop the wall and be on the red, dusty warning track just like hopping the fence around her neighbor's yard. The visitors' bull pen was within shouting distance. And when J.D. Drew took the field for the eighth inning, he'd be standing no more than thirty feet away from her.

Moxie leaned back in the plastic chair and propped her feet on the low wall in front of her, the sun warming her cheeks under the bill of her hat while classic rock pounded through the ballpark's speakers. Dang, she loved Fenway Park.

The score was 1-1, the Sox and Yankees struggling through the hot September afternoon. They were tied for first in the American League East, and a win would mean a place in the playoffs. Okajima—one of Moxie's favorite pitchers—came out to pitch the eighth inning.

Three Yankees batters stepped up . . . and went back down. Moxie yelled "Okieeee!" with the rest of the crowd. She wanted to stand, but splashing around in Lake Melted Dessert was gross. She rocked and bounced in her seat instead. The teenaged guy next to her wrapped his arm around the girl. She brushed him off, leaning forward to see the game better. He scowled and took Moxie's armrest. Moxie rolled her eyes. Fenway was for baseball, not cuddly dates.

The Sox batted. Manny doubled to center field. He waited on second base while David Ortiz came to the plate.

"Papi!" Moxie yelled. Grumps grinned at her.

Moxie held her breath as the Yankees relief pitcher wound up and fired one off. *Fastball, low and away,* read the scoreboard. Papi didn't even flinch, and the ump called ball one. Moxie rubbed the back of her neck. Staring straight ahead, she actually faced the center field scoreboard, screen, and the bleachers. To see home plate, she had to swivel her neck or body to the left.

"The seats don't line up right," Grumps grumbled. "Built it crooked in 1912; we've been payin' for it and fixing stuff ever since. Just watch the pitcher release, then look at the screen to see the call." He held out a long, bony finger, swiping it from pitcher to center field, to show her what he meant. That was easier—but all that head twisting was like watching a tennis match, not baseball.

Next to her, the Dating Couple were snuggling more than game-watching. The girl had painted her nails red and blue, alternating the colors. Each middle fingernail featured a white Boston "B". Moxie was impressed with her dedication, even though she thought nail polish was stupid. The boyfriend, on the other hand, seemed bored by the game. He kept checking his watch and shifting around, and even bumped Moxie's arm twice. She glared at him, but he either didn't notice her or pretended not to. Annoying.

At home plate, Ortiz took two more balls and fouled off another pitch. Moxie leaned forward, arms on the wall, toes on either side of the ice cream, and crossed her fingers. The windup. The release. Papi swung like he wanted to hit tomorrow's moon . . . and the catcher stood behind him, holding the ball. One out.

4

Mike Lowell and J.D. Drew didn't do any better. The eighth inning wound down with Manny stranded at second the whole time.

It was between the eighth and ninth that Grumps left the seats. "Going to run to the gents," Grumps said, giving her shoulder a squeeze. "You know the rule." She nodded and pulled her knees to her chest to let him by. There were lots of family rules, but only one Fenway rule: don't leave the seat by yourself.

Moxie wasn't going anywhere.

Francona sent Okajima out to start the ninth. The first Yankee batter—a real hotshot—made it to second. The crowd, which had been cheering for Okajima and hooting and booing the Yanks, went silent.

"You just never know what those New Yorkers are capable of," Nini, Moxie's grandmother, would say. She hated coming to the park for late season games—said it made her too nervous. But Moxie knew she'd be pacing in front of the TV at home, wearing her old Jim Rice jersey and shouting at the screen like the players could hear her.

Francona popped out of the dugout and took his time crossing to the pitcher's mound. Moxie fidgeted in the seat, trying not to second guess why the manager was leaving Okajima in. "He's got a good reason," she whispered to herself. "A good reason."

Okie struck the next two batters out.

Alex Rodriguez was up. He was Moxie's least favorite player and very dangerous at bat.

"Get him out!" she yelled, unable to control herself.

"Yeah!" Fingernails shouted. Bored Boyfriend looked at his watch again. Why would she even bring this guy to a game? Moxie thought. Why waste a good seat?

Moxie hopped up, right into the ice cream, as Okajima readied the pitch.

The pitch flew. The bat never moved. Strike one.

Moxie hopped back and forth from foot to foot, trying to relax, sneakers sticking to the concrete. "Yeah, Okie!" she cried.

The windup and pitch. Moxie's breath caught in her chest as the ball *popped!* against the bat. The ball flew straight up, then arced behind home plate. Foul. Strike two.

Now everyone, not just Moxie, was on their feet.

Almost everyone: not Bored Boyfriend.

Seriously? Moxie thought.

Rhythmic clapping filled Fenway. "Strike him oowwwt!" she shouted. Dimly, she realized that Grumps still hadn't come back to the seats. Sneaking a cigarette under the bleachers, she thought. Close games made him nervous.

Okajima stepped down from the mound to collect himself. At the plate, A-Rod swung his bat in a tight circle, shaking off his own nerves.

Okajima approached the mound again. Set.

The windup. The release.

The clapping grew louder, faster.

6

Moxie gripped the wall. She kept her eyes on the center field screen, too stressed to watch it live. Curve ball, down and away. Ball one. She exhaled, twisted her neck from side to side, rolled her shoulders.

The clapping began again, filling the park with the sound of giant boots marching. *Clap . . . clap . . . clap . . . clap.* Moxie couldn't join in. Her hands bunched under her chin, shoulders tucked around her ears. She rocked back and forth on the balls of her feet, not even caring about the puddle anymore.

The windup. The pitch. Moxie squinched her eyes closed and peered at the screen through slitted lids.

A-Rod swung from his heels. *CRACK!* The sound echoed through Fenway. The clapping stopped.

Silence.

The ball flew off the bat, screaming into the air. Every pair of eyes in the park watched, tracking its progress across the infield. It pulled right, and a split second later J.D. Drew started moving. Moxie realized that the ball was coming straight for the seats. Her seat.

Time slowed.

Next to her, Long Nails nudged her boyfriend. He was paying attention now. J.D. powered across the outfield, glove outstretched.

Arms still tucked under her chin, feet planted in the ice cream, Moxie felt frozen, trapped in her own body. She couldn't even hear the crowd. She was pretty sure that all 39,000 people in the park were holding their breath, afraid

A-Rod had hit a home run at her head. She struggled through the nightmarish sensation.

Then two realizations: one, the ball was going to fall just short of the seats—J.D. could actually catch it, saving both her and the game, and moving the Sox into the bottom of the ninth with some momentum.

The other? That Mr. Bored Boyfriend wanted the ball as a souvenir for Long Nails. Moxie knew the rules—if this guy leaned over the wall and caught it, it'd be called fan interference. A-Rod would automatically be given a ground rule double—scoring Mr. Hotshot Yankee and giving A-Rod the satisfaction of getting on base.

Boyfriend leaned over, eyes to the sky, hands extended. Since he was in the seats, he had nearly two feet on J.D. Drew.

The ball began its descent, dropping perfectly over her seat. Everyone watched. Moxie knew the camera was on her. J.D. reached the wall, flipped his hat off to see better, jumped.

Boyfriend leaned.

Moxie waited in her World of Slow Motion.

The ball touched the tips of Boyfriend's fingers. As it did so, Moxie did the only thing she could think of: she elbowed him "smack in his privacy," as Nini would say. He doubled over.

And as he cringed, the ball continued to fall, nesting into J.D. Drew's glove with a satisfying *THWOCK!*

The first base umpire, huffing across the field, shouted, "Fair catch! Out!"

Before he spun back to the infield, Drew tossed the ball to Moxie. And winked.

Grumps came back to the seats after Ms. Long Nails and Bored Boyfriend left for the medical station.

"Long line, punkin' pie," he said, smelling of cigarettes and beer. "That's my girl," he added, admiring the ball she turned over and over in her hands.

Moxie smiled and settled into her seat for the last of the ninth, her sneakers leaving sticky waffle prints on the wall.